The

W9-BZA-864

School

TRUE
GHOST
STORIES

First published in 2002 by Usborne Publishing Ltd,
Usborne House, 83-85 Saffron Hill, London
EC1N 8RT, England.
www.usborne.com

A catalogue record for this title is available from
the British Library

UK ISBN 07460 5191 3

First published in America 2004
American ISBN 07945 0274 1

Printed in Great Britain

Based on *Tales of Real Haunting* by Tony Allan
Edited by Paul Dowswell
Series editors: Jane Chisholm & Rosie Dickins
Designed by Brian Voakes
Series designer: Mary Cartwright
Cover design by Glen Bird
Cover image © E.O. Hoppé/Corbis
Digital manipulation by John Russell

TRUE
GHOST
STORIES

Paul Dowswell & Tony Allan

CONTENTS

True stories?

The first detailed account of a haunting, complete with an ancient apparition dragging clanking chains behind it, was put down in writing by a Roman author almost 2,000 years ago. Since then, ghost stories have been told by people all over the world. These include accounts of hauntings by the spirits of people who are still alive, as well as hauntings by the dead. Today, research suggests that around one in ten people claim to have seen a ghost, which adds up to a figure of many millions worldwide. Still, many more haven't, and plenty of them are all too ready to insist that ghosts don't exist.

So how 'true' are the hauntings described in this book? Certainly, the people who witnessed the stories claimed they were true. Among these witnesses were well-respected, educated individuals such as doctors, clergymen and magistrates, all of whom could find no natural explanation for the weird things they saw. In many cases their stories are particularly compelling because they opened themselves up to professional ridicule by insisting they had witnessed supernatural events.

Of course it is always possible that the witnesses in

this book did not have all the facts, or simply mistook a natural phenomenon for a supernatural one. There's no such thing as a guaranteed ghost. And, oddly enough, the very uncertainty surrounding their reports may be what gives tales of hauntings their lasting appeal.

Did Lord Tyrone really come back from the dead to keep a promise to his sister? Was the poison that killed Jack Bell in 19th-century Tennessee really administered by a phantom hand? Were the moving coffins of Barbados actually shifted by restless spirits? This book doesn't claim to have the answers. Instead, it tells the tales as they were reported at the time. It's up to you to decide for yourself whether or not these extraordinary stories are 'true'.

The Vengeful Voodoo Phantom

The grand residence named Rose Hall had never been the same since the grisly death of its mistress, Annie Palmer. In the months after her murder, guests came to the Jamaican mansion house to offer their sympathies to the surviving members of the Palmer family. But at day's end, after they had admired the beautiful views over the island's famous Montego Bay, these guests would sometimes see a strange, ghostly figure drifting up the Hall's grand staircase – a figure that looked oddly familiar. Perhaps it had greeted them on the road to the Hall, beckoning them to come inside?

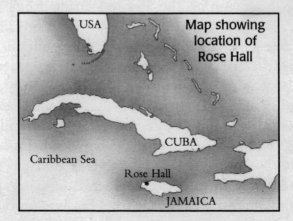

Map showing location of Rose Hall

USA

Caribbean Sea

CUBA

Rose Hall

JAMAICA

Then, at night, as they slept, safe and snug between their cool cotton sheets, these guests would be thrown suddenly from their beds. They would wake with a terrifying sensation — that of having their mattresses pressed down upon them, as if to crush and smother the life out of them. It was all too reminiscent of Annie Palmer's own untimely and unpleasant demise.

❖

In 1800, Rose Hall had been Jamaica's most impressive address. The grand mansion, built in the style of an English stately home, was the residence of the wealthy Palmer family. The Palmers were planters, who had made their fortune off the back of slave workers, who toiled under the blazing Caribbean sun, cutting sugar cane on Rose Hall's vast plantation.

The huge profits the Palmers made from their sugar business helped furnish Rose Hall in magnificent style, and fitted it out with all the luxuries the age could provide. It was here, under the glow of flaming torches, that Jamaica's wealthy elite met at splendid balls and banquets. Gentlemen in powdered wigs and ladies in richly embroidered gowns would dance until dawn, and feast on sumptuous meals served at tables glittering with silver. All around them was evidence of the Palmer family's fabulous wealth, for the Hall was festooned with hand-tooled carvings, intricate plasterwork and magnificent paintings.

❖

But all this was to change. By the time the century was halfway through, Rose Hall would be a crumbling shadow of its former glory. Tropical vegetation invaded the imposing drive up to the house, and choked the once carefully-tended flower beds. Weeds and moss grew in cracks on the pillared terrace, and bats and toads made their homes in rooms where dancers had once spun. And if a visitor should ask what had caused the house to fall into ruin, they were told it was all the work of one woman – evil Annie Palmer.

This was undoubtedly true. The seeds of the house's destruction lay in John Rose Palmer's decision to marry Annie, a fiery Irish girl who had been brought up on the nearby island of Haiti. John was head of the Palmer family, so his new bride became mistress of Rose Hall. She was only 18 years old.

Annie was petite and beautiful, but she had a sharp tongue and would fly into a raging temper if she could not get her own way. Almost as soon as she arrived, she became feared and hated by the staff and servants of the Hall, who would gossip incessantly about her terrible conduct. One story about her swept through the servants like wildfire. It was said that when she was a child, her Haitian nurse had taught her the art of voodoo – Haiti's secret and sinister witchcraft religion.

But this piece of gossip was as nothing compared to what was whispered when John Palmer passed away, only a few months after the couple's marriage. Officially, it was said that John had died after eating some poisonous shellfish. But on the night of his death, servants had heard a terrible argument between John and Annie. Straining to hear the couple as they raged and fought, a chambermaid heard John accuse Annie of taking a handsome slave as a lover. He told her that their marriage was over, and that she should leave Rose Hall the following morning.

But the next morning came and went. Annie had appeared as usual for breakfast, but she seemed slightly subdued, and told the staff her husband was ill and wished to be left alone.

That evening a servant had gone to his master's bedroom to find John Palmer stone cold dead, his face contorted in an agonizing grimace. The Hall staff immediately decided Annie must have poisoned him, but the doctor called to examine the body was sure his demise was due to the seafood he had eaten the night before. Perhaps Annie had used a secret voodoo recipe to poison him? Whatever she might have done, she had covered her tracks very carefully.

Then, over the next few days, more gossip drifted

in from the plantation. It appeared that one of the slaves had indeed been seeing Annie. It was even whispered that this slave had helped to murder John Palmer, by smothering him with a pillow as he lay groaning in his bed, in agony from the poison that coursed through his body. When Annie ordered that this same slave should be whipped to death for a trivial wrongdoing only she had witnessed, tongues began to wag even louder. It looked as if Annie had decided to remove the only other witness to John Palmer's murder, so that no one could ever accuse her of causing his death.

❖

With her husband dead and buried, Annie Palmer was now a very wealthy woman, and the sole mistress of Rose Hall. She had friends at the highest level of Jamaican society, and no one at the Hall ever dared openly voice their suspicion that Annie had murdered her husband. She would marry twice more, and in both cases her husbands would die suspiciously young and unexpectedly. Again, servants were convinced that they had been discarded when Annie grew tired of them. But, as before, nothing could be proven, and it seemed that no one dared mention their concerns to the police.

The staff of the Hall had much to put up with in Annie's tyrannous whims and fancies, but it was the slaves on the plantation who suffered the most. She would sometimes pluck a handsome slave from the fields and take him as her lover. But after a while she grew bored, and he would simply disappear. Women slaves who met with her disapproval were beaten with a wooden rod until their bare backs bled. Sometimes, she would gallop around the plantation with a whip, and mercilessly lash out at any slave who crossed her path.

❖

Some time in 1833 the delicate balance between fear and hatred tipped to Annie's disadvantage. Inside the Hall, a slave she was whipping finally snapped. In desperation, he turned around and grabbed her by the throat. Her muffled screams for help were heard by other slaves nearby, but instead of rescuing their cruel mistress, they helped finish her off. Rose Hall's slaves had learned a trick or two in their time on the plantation. If Annie was murdered, a culprit would be found and hanged. So if their mistress was to be killed, they knew it had to be done with great cunning, so as not to leave a shred of evidence. Annie Palmer's final moments came when she was wedged hard beneath a mattress and smothered to death. Then her body was laid carefully down on the floor. The doctor who saw her thought she had had a seizure, and could find no marks on her body to indicate she had been attacked.

She was hated so much that no one at the Hall

would arrange her burial, and although it was an open secret that she had been murdered, no one took this story to the police. Eventually, Annie Palmer's fellow plantation owners arranged her funeral, and she was buried in a plot in the extensive grounds of the Hall.

It was soon after this that strange stories started to spread, and none were more terrifying, or were more often told, than the strange, vivid dreams visitors had of being smothered by mattresses. Although the plantation continued to be run by the surviving members of the Palmer family, none of them wanted to live in the Hall. So nature took its course. Vegetation covered the grounds, and tiles fell from the roof. Mildew spread over the bedroom walls and the furnishings were looted. As the years went by, so Rose Hall fell into dereliction.

Even then, the family employed a caretaker to try to protect their once grand mansion. But when he was found dead at the bottom of the cellar steps, people whispered that it was no accident. They were sure that he had fallen to his death, fleeing in panic from the ghost of Annie Palmer.

❖

For nearly a hundred years the huge Hall lay completely deserted. The wind whistled through broken windows and the rain trickled down through the rotten plaster of the walls and ceilings. Anyone who was foolhardy enough to trespass inside the building often came away with a feeling of inexplicable dread.

Over the years, attempts were made to bring peace to the house by laying the ghost of Annie Palmer to rest. In 1952, a famous American medium named Eileen Garret paid four visits to the Hall, seeking to make contact with Annie. Witnesses say she succeeded.

On one terrifying occasion, it was reported that Annie spoke through the body of Eileen Garret, uttering this terrible threat: "Let no one think this is the end of me... My shrieks will live and those that seek to inherit this Hall will find a curse upon them."

It was not a promising sign. Eileen Garret decided that Annie Palmer's ghost should be left undisturbed.

Nonetheless, nearly 30 years later, a group of mediums returned to Rose Hall to try to contact Annie again. A crowd of around 8,000 sensation-seeking tourists and locals also came along to witness their work. This time, it seemed, Annie was in a better mood.

One medium reported that the ghost had given her a message that led them to a huge termites' nest behind the mansion. Here, they found an old brass vase containing a doll in a paper gown, of a type used in voodoo ceremonies. The vase and its contents were removed and destroyed, and the mediums and the crowd left, hoping that peace would finally be restored to haunted Rose Hall.

Afterwards

Perhaps the mediums did their work well, for the Rose Hall story has a happy ending. Peace did return to the ruined mansion, which was bought by an American millionaire. He was not remotely bothered by tales of hauntings and curses, and he spent a great deal of money restoring the house to its former glory.

Today Rose Hall is a popular tourist spot, visited by thousands of people every year. They come to admire the carefully tended tropical gardens, and gawp at Rose Hall's sumptuous interior. But, most of all, they come to hear the chilling tale of its former haunting, and witness the site of the fiendish deeds of its one-time mistress, evil Annie Palmer.

The Cock Lane Killing

Richard Parsons would live to regret the moment he he first met William Kent – but in the early days of their friendship the two men were almost as close as brothers. Parsons lived in a narrow backstreet called Cock Lane, near to St. Paul's Cathedral in the heart of London. One October day in 1759, he was working as an usher at his local church of St. Sepulchre's. Here he met Kent, a stranger in the area, who was looking for lodgings for himself and his partner, Fanny.

Parsons invited the couple to move in with his family, and Kent seized the opportunity. The two of them got along so well that Kent even lent his new landlord money. He also confessed his greatest secret – he and Fanny Lynes, the woman he lived with, were not married. Fanny, who was expecting his child, was the sister of his previous wife, who had died in childbirth. By a strange quirk in the law at the time, it was forbidden for a widowed husband to marry his wife's sister. After his bereavement, Fanny and Kent had fallen in love. They were now living together as man and wife. This was a shocking state of affairs in 18th-century England.

After some weeks at Cock Lane, Kent had to go away on business. During this time, Fanny shared a room with the Parsons' 11-year-old daughter, Elizabeth. It was then that the family began to feel that their house might be haunted.

One morning, Fanny came downstairs looking exhausted.

"Whatever is the matter?" asked Mrs. Parsons. "Did you not sleep?"

Fanny looked pained. "I heard bangings and thumpings all through the night," she said. "I almost came to believe that this house was haunted..."

Mrs. Parsons laughed. "Why, that will be the shoemaker next door. He has a workshop in the house."

"But last night was Sunday night, Mrs. Parsons. Nobody works on Sunday night."

An uneasy silence fell between them. Mrs. Parsons had to admit it was rather odd.

❖

It was some time after this that the Kents began to fall out with their landlord and his family. Parsons failed to repay Kent the money he had borrowed. Kent in turn began to think this was because he had been foolish enough to tell him that Fanny was not really his wife. Nonetheless, this did not stop Kent from threatening Parsons with a law suit, if Parsons did not repay him. Parsons retaliated by telling everyone he knew that the Kents were not really married. They moved out of Cock Lane soon after, their friendship with the Parsons family irredeemably ruined.

Shortly after their departure, Richard Parsons' house became the scene of regular and highly unusual disturbances. At night, the whole family became aware of frequent and inexplicable rustlings and bangings. Then, one night, they saw a brilliant white light rushing up the stairs. A friend, who was visiting at the time, said it was bright enough to light up a clock across the street.

But ghostly bangings were nothing compared to the troubles that befell William Kent and Fanny Lynes, who were now living in nearby Clerkenwell. Fanny, who was now heavily pregnant, had fallen ill with a disease that was diagnosed as smallpox. She fought grimly for her life, but died barely a month after leaving Cock Lane. Her body was buried in the vaults of the local church of St. John's.

❖

News of the tragedy gradually filtered back to the Parsons. They couldn't help noticing that, after Fanny's death, there seemed to be a pause in the noises heard in Cock Lane. But a year later they came back louder than ever. And this time, they were clearly connected to Elizabeth Parsons, now 13. Bizarrely, the strange banging sounds only seemed to occur in her presence.

The parents sought some rational explanation for the noises. They asked the shoemaker next door to let them know when he was working. They even hired a carpenter to take down panels around the wall of Elizabeth's bedroom, in case rats, or some other hidden cause, might be responsible. But nothing was found. Gradually, reluctantly, they came to the conclusion that the noises must be supernatural. Perhaps a local clergyman could help?

The man they approached was the Reverend John Moore, a well respected local figure. He visited the house and quickly became convinced that the knocking noises were made by a ghost. He talked with the ghost as if it where there in the room before him, and suggested they have a conversation.

"One knock will mean 'yes', and two knocks will mean 'no'!" he exclaimed.

Using this rather laborious method of communication, the ghostly knocker made some startling revelations. It let the Reverend Moore know that it was the spirit of Fanny Lynes, and that it wanted the world to know that she had been murdered.

Moore was joined by Parsons, who listened wide-eyed to Fanny Lynes' tragic tale. After a great deal of speculation and guesswork by the two men, they discovered that William Kent had killed Fanny by putting the poison arsenic in a glass of purl – a medicinal drink that was popular at the time. It was commonly known that arsenic was supposed to be a perfect poison for murders, as its presence in the body was difficult to detect. Moore and Parsons also established that Fanny thought that Kent had killed her so he could get his hands on her savings, and also because he did not want to have to support the baby she was expecting.

❖

London in the 18th century was a bustling city of coffee houses and coaching inns, where gossip spread through teeming streets and crowded alleys like wildfire. Before long the story of the ghost, and its accusations of murder, appeared in a local newspaper. A copy of the paper was shown to William Kent. Although he was not mentioned by name, he knew at once that the story was about him. Fearing he might be lynched by an angry mob, he went at once to Cock Lane, intending to clear his name.

He spoke at length with the Reverend Moore, who suggested he talk directly with the spirit. The fateful encounter took place on January 12, 1762. Word had spread around the whole district, and the tiny bedroom where Elizabeth usually slept was crowded with spectators. After some delay, knockings were finally heard, indicating that the ghost was now ready to proceed.

Moore stepped forward to put his questions to the invisible spirit.

"Are you the wife of Mr. Kent?" he asked.

Back came two knocks for 'No', but by then everyone knew that Kent and Fanny Lynes had not been married.

"Did you die naturally?" asked Moore.

Two knocks.

A buzz of excitement shot around the room, and Moore had to hold up his hand to silence the onlookers.

"Were you poisoned?" the clergyman asked.

One knock followed – meaning 'Yes'.

"Did any person other than Mr. Kent administer it?" said Moore.

Two knocks.

Kent could feel a noose tightening round his neck. As superstitious and ignorant as everyone else in the room, he had no doubt he was talking to a real ghost. Now, the room was in uproar, and he felt at once that he was in very serious trouble. Especially when one of the spectators shouted out another question.

"Will Mr. Kent be hanged for your murder?"

One knock followed.

Kent could take no more, and flew into a rage. "This ghost is a plain liar," he thundered, "or mistakes me for another gentleman. I would never have murdered my dear Fanny, and I am dumbfounded that you should subject me to such humiliation while I still grieve for my departed wife, and the child that she carried."

He turned and left. The crowd had been so

astounded by his violent speech that they parted before him to let him go.

❖

News of the ghostly confrontation soon made the Cock Lane haunting the talk of London. In the days that followed, Elizabeth Parson's bedroom was filled to bursting with spectators hoping for fresh revelations. So many people turned up at the house that the road outside was regularly blocked by onlookers.

Richard Parsons reasoned that such upheaval was not good for his house and family, so Elizabeth was moved to a larger house nearby. The knocking duly moved with her, and so did the crowds. By now, even fashionable society figures such as the Duke of York, King George III's brother, had begun to seek out Elizabeth Parsons and the eerie knocking that she seemed to attract.

After 11 days of mounting chaos, the Lord Mayor of London was told that something would have to be done to calm the crowds. Hoping to find some logical explanation for the phenomenon, the Mayor announced that the affair would be investigated by a committee of eminent men. Among them would be Dr. Samuel Johnson, author of the first English dictionary, who agreed to prepare the official report.

The committee began their investigations on February 1, 1762. For the Parsons family, it was a disaster. Confronted with an unfriendly audience of learned men, the spirit resolutely refused to put in an appearance. Then an earlier claim it was reported to have made, that it would bang on Fanny Lynes coffin, was put to the test. Sometime after midnight on February 2, Elizabeth Parsons was taken to the crypt of St. John's, Clerkenwell, and stood before Fanny's coffin. An expectant silence ensued, but that was all that happened. Johnson and his committee concluded that an increasingly flustered Elizabeth Parsons had faked the whole haunting.

But that was not the end of it. In the days that followed, wherever Elizabeth went, knockings were heard louder than ever. She was moved from house to house, and odd events were noted wherever she went. In one place a loose curtain ring was seen to spin around on its rail, and the bangings became so violent that terrified residents asked her to leave and not come back.

Finally, a fresh committee of investigation decided to resolve the situation by placing Elizabeth under strict surveillance. She was taken to a house in Covent Garden, where a maid shared her bed, keeping hold of her arms and legs throughout the night. Still, the knockings continued. Over the next few nights, Elizabeth was placed in a hammock, with her arms and legs tied together. This time, the ghost fell silent.

The next night, Elizabeth was subjected to a transparently unfair trick by the committee. She was not tied up while she slept, but told instead that if no knockings were heard both she and her parents would be sent to prison. Then, she was left on her own.

A peephole had been drilled in the wall, and she was closely watched by members of the committee throughout the night. After a couple of hours, an observer saw her tiptoe out of bed, and over to the fireplace. Here, she picked up a block of wood. Then she took it back to her bed, and was later heard to knock on it.

All those present in the house who had heard the previous ghostly knockings agreed that this noise sounded quite different. Nonetheless, Elizabeth's pitiful attempt to keep her family out of prison was taken as conclusive proof that the entire haunting was nothing but a fraud.

❖

The authorities decided Elizabeth's parents had been responsible for the whole charade. They were put on trial, found guilty, and sent to prison. As an additional punishment, Richard Parsons was sentenced to stand in the pillory three times. This was a wooden post set up to hold a criminal, where passers-by could throw stones or rotten vegetables at him.

The Reverend Moore was seen by the court as Parsons' accomplice. He was not sent to jail, but instead was ordered to pay William Kent a large sum of money in compensation. Kent, of course, was delighted. By this time he had remarried, and was now a successful stockbroker.

But, despite the court's findings, many people sympathized with Richard Parsons. When the time came for him to stand in the pillory, he was not pelted with vegetables. Rather, the reverse happened, and onlookers took up a collection for him.

After that, the story came to an end. There were no more ghostly knockings. Whatever people may have thought on the streets, rich and influential Londoners accepted the court's judgment without question. The Cock Lane haunting, it was agreed, was one of the greatest shams ever. The story went down in London's folklore, to be repeated endlessly in taverns and storybooks.

Afterwards

There was to be an intriguing footnote to the Cock Lane haunting. Almost a century later, an artist named J.W. Archer went to visit the church of St. John's, where Fanny Lynes was laid to rest. He found the vault in disarray, with coffins, and even corpses, lying jumbled around the floor.

A boy who knew the church well had accompanied him, and pointed out a coffin that was said to be that of the infamous Fanny Lynes. Archer knew the story well. Overcome with curiosity, he gingerly prized open the lid. It did indeed contain the body of a woman. But there were no signs of the smallpox she was supposed to have died from. Instead, the features were unusually well preserved — which, as Archer realized, is typical of corpses affected by arsenic poisoning.

Writing on the Wall

Esther Cox was a troublesome teenager. But, no wonder, for she had seen a great deal of sadness and turmoil in her short life. Her mother had died when she was still a young child. Then her father had remarried. His new wife did not like Esther, nor her younger sister Jane. The two girls were packed off to live with their Aunt Olive and her husband in remote Amherst, on the snow-bound coast of Nova Scotia, in Canada.

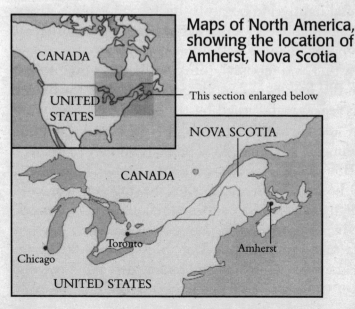

Maps of North America, showing the location of Amherst, Nova Scotia

CANADA

UNITED STATES

This section enlarged below

NOVA SCOTIA

CANADA

Toronto

Amherst

Chicago

UNITED STATES

Aunt Olive and her husband, Daniel Teed, had two young children themselves. They all lived together in a wooden cottage with four rooms on each floor. Esther and Jane settled in uneasily, but Esther, especially, was a difficult child to like. Now 16, she was a short, moon-faced girl with a nasty temper, who would sulk for hours if she did not get her own way.

Esther had a boyfriend in the town named Bob McNeal. He was also less than charming, as Esther found out one summer night in 1878. Esther and Bob were out riding on Bob's horse-drawn buggy. Somewhere outside the town he stopped and told her to go into the woods with him. Esther refused, and slapped his face. Bob McNeal did not take her refusal lightly. He began to hit her, and shout at her. Then he pulled out a pistol, and ordered her at gunpoint to come with him.

Esther was terrified, thinking he was going to kill her. But luckily, before she got down from the buggy, McNeal was disturbed by the sound of a horse and cart approaching. Furiously, he grabbed the reins of the buggy, and turned his horse round.

Bob and Esther drove back to Amherst in silence, he boiling with rage, she shaking in fear and indignation. As if to add to their misery and anger, the heavens opened and both were soaked to the skin in a terrific downpour. Bob McNeal left Esther on her doorstep, drenched and bedraggled. He drove off, never to be seen in Amherst again.

Always something of a secretive child, Esther told no one of her ordeal, keeping her own fear and rage locked up inside her. For a week or so she went around red-eyed and tearful, and everyone just assumed she and Bob had argued. But seven days after the incident, something very strange occurred in the Teed household. It was the start of an ordeal that would last for over two years.

❖

Esther and Jane shared a bed. One night, after they had turned out their oil lamp and were both drifting off to sleep, Esther suddenly leaped out of the bed.

"There's a mouse! Wriggling around under the sheets!" she yelled.

Jane got out of bed, and relit the oil lamp. She turned back the bedsheets and both girls peered at the mattress. Both of them thought they could see something stirring in the mattress, but it seemed to be inside it, where they couldn't get at it. They waited, shivering in the cold and straining to see in the dull yellow glow of the lamp. But nothing else happened, so they remade the bed and went back to sleep.

The next night, they had almost forgotten about the incident, but then they were disturbed by a rustling under the bed.

"It's that mouse again," giggled Jane, and once again they lit the oil lamp.

This time, the noise seemed to be coming from a cardboard box filled with patchwork pieces. They pulled it out into the middle of the room, preparing to empty it out and chase off whatever was inside it. But instead, to their amazement, the whole box shot up high into the air, emptying patchwork pieces all over the room. They were both astounded, but not yet frightened. Jane set the box back in the middle of the floor, but exactly the same thing happened again. At this point both girls screamed, and their Uncle Daniel rushed into the room to see what was happening.

"The box is bouncing into the air. Uncle Dan, you must believe us. It happened twice, just now," said Esther.

Daniel Teed was more amused than anything else. "You girls must have been dreaming – or playing silly beggars. Now pick up those pieces, and put the box back under the bed."

The next day at breakfast, the Teeds joked about the box, and the girls themselves even began to wonder if they hadn't just imagined it all.

❖

But everything fell into place on the next day, and Esther soon came to realize that the goings on of the previous nights had been a prelude to something far worse. That evening she went to bed early, complaining of feeling ill. But shortly after Jane came to join her, Esther suddenly flung herself out of bed, pulling all the blankets with her.

"What's happening to me?" she shouted, panic in her eyes. "I'm dying."

Jane lit their oil lamp, and was horrified at what she saw. Esther's eyes were bulging, and her face had turned bright red. Most bizarrely, all her hair was standing on end.

Jane called for help, and soon the entire family had rushed into the room. At first they thought Esther had gone insane. They tried to get her to go back into her bed, but as soon as she lay down she started to swell up like a balloon. Her skin was burning hot, and she was screaming in pain.

No one in the room doubted they were witnessing her final agonizing death-throes, but then there was a vast crashing sound, like a gigantic peal of thunder. Everyone stopped, and stood frozen in horror. Three more crashes followed. While the rest of the family stood staring at each other in amazement, Esther suddenly seemed to relax. Her body returned to its normal size, her temperature cooled down, and she just lay in her bed, fast asleep, as if nothing extraordinary had happened at all.

Three nights of peace followed, but then the whole drama was repeated, only this time the bedsheets kept flying off the bed and sailing over to a far corner of the room. Some of the Teed family leaped after them, and had to sit on them to hold them down. Once again the whole episode came to an end with a series of loud thundery bangs.

Daniel Teed realized then that Esther needed some serious help. The family doctor, Dr. Carritte, agreed to visit the house the next evening.

Ghosts and poltergeists often refrain from performing when their victims are being observed by others. But not this time. Dr. Carritte examined Esther closely, and the two of them had a quiet chat. Then the doctor gathered Mr. and Mrs. Teed around the bedside and began to explain that, in his opinion, Esther was suffering from nervous excitement — a common complaint for girls of her age. She should get plenty of rest, and avoid anything that brought on anxiety.

But even as he talked, and Esther's aunt and uncle nodded sagely, a pillow behind the bed slid silently out from under the girl's head and floated up into the air like a balloon. Then it slipped neatly back into place, as if nothing had happened.

The doctor was standing open-mouthed when the same thing happened again. This time Daniel Teed grabbed the pillow but, even though he pulled with all his strength, he could not stop it from sliding back.

Then a strange banging began. It seemed to be coming from under the bed. Dr. Carritte bent down, but could see nothing unusual. As he got up, the noise seemed to move in his direction. Aghast, he retreated to the door, and an eerie thumping followed him all the way. Then the blankets flew off the bed.

At this moment, with the rest of the Teed family dashing hysterically around the room trying to retrieve the blankets, another sound filled the room. This was a more sinister scraping noise, which seemed to be coming from the wall directly above the bed.

All at once a message appeared on the wall, in letters a foot high. They looked as if they had been carved in the plaster by a metal spike. The words filled everyone in the room with a livid terror, and none more so than poor Esther, for they read:

ESTHER COX YOU ARE MINE TO KILL

There was more to come. As Dr. Carritte stood transfixed, staring at the writing in astonishment, a piece of plaster detached itself from the wall, and hurled itself at him. Then it came to an abrupt halt, and landed at his feet.

The banging started again, this time loud enough to shake the whole room. The noise continued for a couple of hours and only stopped when Esther fell into an exhausted sleep.

Dr. Carritte returned to visit Esther the next day. This time he was pelted with potatoes that seemed just to fly out of nowhere, and he fled from the house. That night, the banging returned louder than ever. It seemed as if someone was pounding on the wooden tiles of the roof with a sledgehammer.

❖

By now, the noises and the strange goings on had attracted the attention of others in the street. Soon, Esther Cox was the talk of Amherst. People flocked to the house in the hope of observing something strange happening, and sometimes the crowds were so unruly that the police had to be called to control them.

Esther's troubles continued, although the ghostly presence that tormented her seemed to stick to just banging, rather than anything more dramatic. Then she fell ill with diphtheria. Curiously, the phantom took no interest in tormenting the seriously ill girl, and peace returned to the Teed household. Esther took several months to recover from this illness, and the family enjoyed a quiet Christmas. They were looking forward to a trouble-free New Year, but it was not to be...

Almost as soon as Esther had recovered from her illness, odd things began to happen. This time, they took a decidedly dangerous turn. One night, as they lay in bed together, Esther woke Jane in a panic and told her that she had just heard a ghostly voice telling her it intended to set the house on fire.

Jane had seen enough of Esther's phantom tormentor to know that serious trouble was afoot. She ran out onto the landing, and shouted for the rest of the family to wake up. But Mr. and Mrs. Teed refused to take Esther's warning seriously.

Mr. Teed seemed exasperated. "Ghosts can't start fires, Esther. Surely you know that?"

But, just as he spoke, a lighted match appeared from nowhere, up near to the ceiling, and fell onto the bed. Jane quickly put it out, but for the next ten minutes the family ran around in a hysterical flurry, extinguishing the succession of blazing matches that fell onto their furniture.

News of this latest outrage at the Teed household caused a panic in the town, as all the houses there were made of wood. It was the middle of winter and, in the strong winter gales that blow particularly hard in that part of Canada, a fire in one house could spread quickly to another. A devastating fire in an isolated, remote community could destroy every means of shelter – and at that time of year, such a prospect didn't even bear thinking about.

❖

A few days later, the town mayor took Daniel Teed to one side as he walked down the high street. The mayor quietly suggested that perhaps Esther would be less troubled by the ghost if she went to live somewhere else. Daniel was affronted, saying he had treated the girl as if she were his own daughter. The mayor was a patient man, and understood Teed's anger, but told him that people in Amherst were so frightened by the events that had taken place at his house that they were willing to take the law into their own hands.

Teed walked off home full of shame and anger, his eyes staring at the ground lest he catch the hostile gaze of one of his fellow townspeople. What did the mayor mean? Were they planing a lynching, a ransacking of his home, or what? He had no option, he told himself, but to let Esther go.

The next nine months were difficult ones for the troubled teenager. She moved from house to house in Amherst, but everywhere she went, the ghost would follow. There were even fresh torments, to keep her on her toes. Now past school age, Esther worked in a restaurant in the town. Here metal objects such as knives and forks seemed to be drawn to her, as though to a magnet. One time, a boy's pocketknife flew through the air, striking her on the back of the neck and drawing blood. Another time, a shower of pins flew up from a table, and stuck into her body.

Gradually, the power of the poltergeists began to wane, but Esther's run of ill fortune had not finished yet. In July 1879, she went to live with a family named Van Amburgh at a farm outside Amherst. She had few problems here – only the occasional rapping on walls and windows.

While staying with the Van Amburghs, Esther

found a farming job with the Davison family. Unfortunately, things did not work out. The Van Amburghs began to notice that various items of clothing had gone missing from their house. When these were later found in the Davisons' barn, Esther, of course, was accused of stealing them. Before the claims could be investigated further, the barn burned down. Now Esther was accused of both theft and arson. She was put on trial, found guilty, and sentenced to four months in prison. But when several people in the town spoke up for Esther, explaining to the judge that she had had a very tough life, the sentence was reduced to four weeks. The prison spell seemed like a bad thing for Esther at the time, but it turned out for the best. Following her stint in prison, the haunting of Esther Cox came to an end as unaccountably as it had begun.

Afterwards

Esther Cox was destined not to have a happy life. She married twice and had a child, but when a journalist investigating the haunting tracked her down, she was living alone and in squalor. By then in her late 40s, she was so desperate for money that she refused to talk to the journalist unless he gave her $100. It was an offer he turned down.

Esther died five years later at the age of 52. Her story remains genuinely perplexing to investigators of the paranormal. In many ways it was a typical case of a poltergeist haunting. Teenagers are said to be classic targets for such spirits, and some observers have suggested that they have a need to draw on adolescent energies to bring themselves into being. Sometimes, too, adolescents find that a haunting begins after they have had a particularly unpleasant experience. Esther's attack by her boyfriend seems to have triggered her bout of poltergeist activity.

In later years, writers reviewing the case have suggested that she may have faked some of the manifestations. Yet many reliable witnesses were genuinely convinced that they had seen and heard the strangest, most inexplicable things. Esther Cox's haunting cannot be so easily dismissed. Her doctor, for example, wrote about the haunting to a fellow medical professional, five years after the trouble began: "Honest, sceptical persons were on all occasions soon convinced that there was no fraud or deception in the case… I am certain I could not have believed such apparent miracles had I not witnessed them myself."

The House of Strange Happenings

Harper is not the real name of the family in this story, but one chosen by investigators to protect the true identity of those concerned. Their first names have also been changed.

In our imagination, we usually think of hauntings happening in ruined castles or deserted country fields that were once the scene of terrible battles. Ghosts seem to belong in such dramatic and historical locations. Nonetheless, it was an ordinary family house in Enfield, England that became the site of the most thoroughly investigated haunting in modern times.

Enfield lies on the northern outskirts of London – its row upon row of neat brick houses are edged with miniature gardens and tightly parked cars. It was here that the Harper family made their home. Mrs. Harper, who was separated from her husband, shared a house with her four children: Rose, 13, Janet, 11, Peter, 10, and Jimmy, 7. Their lives were a picture of ordinariness and normality – until the haunting began.

One summer evening in August 1977, Peter and Janet, who shared a room, were drifting off to sleep. Suddenly, their beds started to shake. It was almost like the shaking that might be caused by a huge truck driving past the house. The children were startled, and their mother heard them cry out in fright. But Mrs. Harper thought her children were just playing a game. She shouted up the stair, telling them to settle down. Then the shaking stopped and, by the morning, both children had forgotten all about the incident.

The next evening was even odder. As Peter and Janet were settling down for the night, they heard a shuffling noise in their room, as if someone was walking across the floor wearing slippers. Again, they shouted out for Mrs. Harper. There must have been a genuine edge of fear in their voices, for she came running up the stairs. She heard the shuffling as clearly as they did, along with three or four loud knocks.

Then, in front of their startled eyes, a heavy chest of drawers in the bedroom began to move. It slid about 50cm (20in) away from the wall. Mrs. Harper pushed it back again. There was a pause, then it moved forward once more. Again, Mrs. Harper leaned down to push it back against the wall, but this time it would not budge. It was as if someone unseen was pushing as hard as they could on the other side. This was all too much for Mrs. Harper and her terrified children. They fled out onto the street.

Next door, Vic and Peggy Nottingham were getting themselves ready for bed. Vic heard an urgent knocking on their front door. He opened it to see Mrs. Harper, trembling with fear and looking totally bewildered, and her four children, all wearing their dressing gowns and slippers.

Vic was not a great believer in ghosts, and the story Mrs. Harper stammered out seemed rather ridiculous. But he could see how distressed they all were. While Peggy made them hot chocolate, he went into the Harper house to investigate. Climbing the stairs he could detect nothing unusual, and started to feel mildly irritated. But then the knocking started. It seemed to follow him from room to room.

"Must be your central heating, Mrs. Harper," he said when he returned.

"We haven't got central heating," she replied.

Now Vic Nottingham was feeling as foxed as the Harpers. He announced that he was going to call the police.

Ten minutes later, revolving blue lights flashing around the street, a squad car with two policemen pulled up outside the house. While one policeman stayed to talk to the children in the Harper's living room, the other went upstairs with Vic and Mrs. Harper. He seemed amused to be there.

"We don't get many hauntings in Enfield, madam," he said with exaggerated politeness. "Good thing it's a quiet night."

But his smug smile vanished when he heard cries

43

of alarm from the living room. He dashed downstairs, followed closely by Vic and Mrs. Harper. In front of everyone, a chair started to rock from side to side. As they watched in astonishment, it slid toward the kitchen, just as if it were being pushed.

The police stayed with the Harpers until midnight, then left. There was little they could do to help except try to calm the frightened family. Besides, as one of the policemen quietly explained, however odd the happenings in the house, no one was breaking the law.

❖

Over the next four days, more bizarre things started to happen. Marbles and plastic building bricks flew through the air. When touched, they were burning hot. Even more strangely, the marbles did not roll when they hit the ground, but stopped stock-still.

Mrs. Harper's nerves were in shreds. She turned again for advice to her friends next door. Peggy Nottingham, a regular reader of the *Daily Mirror*, one of Britain's most popular tabloid newspapers, suggested she contact the paper. She felt someone there would at least be able to suggest where the family could look for help.

Soon after, a reporter and photographer turned up at the Harper home. Their strange story duly appeared on the front page of the newspaper, under a headline that read "The House of Strange Happenings". The paper also put the family in touch with the Society for Psychical Research (SPR), an organization originally set up in the 1880s to study supernatural events.

The SPR sent Maurice Grosse, one of their researchers, to investigate. He was joined a few days later by an author named Guy Lyon Playfair, who was to write about the Enfield events in his book *This House is Haunted*. Often, when a spirit is faced with independent observers, it hides away, only emerging again to torment its victims when outsiders are safely away. The Enfield spirit, however, was not remotely shy. The presence of the two men sparked a terrifying series of extraordinary events as the house seemed to come under siege from unseen forces.

Over several weeks, heavy items of furniture such as dressers and tables were suddenly flipped over, or moved across the room, as if disturbed by a giant hand. An iron fireplace grille, firmly cemented to the wall, flew across a bedroom, landing a whisker away from the head of a sleeping child. Rose and Janet were regularly flung from their beds, sometimes half a dozen times in a single night.

❖

Playfair decided the answer to this perplexing mystery was to call in several mediums. These are people who claim to have special powers which enable them to communicate with the dead. By attempting to contact the spirits responsible for the haunting, Playfair hoped to discover why they were behaving in this fashion.

All the mediums who came to visit sensed the presence of some supernatural force or being, although each seemed to detect a different one. One medium claimed to have contacted a spirit called Gozer. She described him as "a nasty piece of work". Another medium spoke of an unpleasant old woman who had once lived near London's Spitalfields vegetable market, and had a distinct whiff of rotting vegetables about her. Using the mediums to find a solution was getting the researchers nowhere, and still the haunting continued.

Then events in the house became even more frightening as Janet, and later Rose, started making strange and startling utterances, in a deep, guttural tone. Playfair dubbed these occurrences "The Voice"; he believed the girls had become a living mouthpiece for the spirits involved in the haunting.

On one occasion, one of the girls seemed to go into a trance-like state. Then she announced that she was "Joe Watson", who went on to explain that he was a former tenant who had died in the house some years before. Another time "The Voice" said it was a man called Bill Haylock, who was buried at a local cemetery named Durant's Park.

Playfair was not a credulous man. His intention

from the start was to find some logical explanation for these strange goings-on. He had originally suspected that Janet, an unusually lively girl, might be faking at least some, if not all, of these incidents. On one occasion he caught her hiding his tape recorder in a cupboard, and guessed that she intended him to think that a phantom had whisked it away and left it there. But what he saw in the house during his stay convinced him that very few of the hundreds of strange events he witnessed could be dismissed as childish pranks.

❖

Further, seemingly inexplicable events continued to occur throughout the year the investigators spent on the case. Oddly shaped pools of water appeared from nowhere on the kitchen floor. More alarmingly, fires broke out in closed drawers. But, amazingly, they just burned themselves out inside the drawer and never did much damage. Once, a cardboard box full of cushions took off from the floor, sailed through the air and hit Grosse on the forehead. Another time, Rose was going upstairs when an unseen force seemed to grip her leg. She froze in terror and was only able to move again when another person in the house came to help her.

Janet, meanwhile, was behaving even more bizarrely, and had begun to claim she sometimes floated up to the ceiling during the night. On one occasion, a passer-by looked up at the bedroom window to see books, dolls and other objects circling around the room, with Janet floating alongside them. She looked as though she was in a trance, and occasionally her hand would bang against the window. The passer-by thought she was going to sail straight through the window.

But while the Enfield poltergeist was happy to play its tricks for the Harpers and Grosse and Playfair, it refused to allow them to record any of its activity. Playfair came to believe that it was cunning enough to want to protect itself from observation, almost as though it were playing a game in which it sought to win attention without having its secrets discovered. It certainly seemed to be able to jinx recording equipment: at different times, cameras, tape recorders and video equipment all inexplicably failed to perform.

The haunting then moved into another phase, and reached a peak when people in the house started to see phantoms, as well as hear them and witness their activity. First, a hollow appeared on a pillow, like that made by the head of a small child. Then Mrs. Harper saw what appeared to be part of a ghost – just the bottom half of an old-fashioned pair of men's trousers moving up the stairs.

A friend of the family named John Burcombe came to visit, and got an even fuller view of the phantom. It was wearing a 1930s-style shirt with no collar, and a pair of black trousers. It sat perfectly still, looking away from the visitor. Burcombe closed his eyes briefly in disbelief and, when he opened them, the figure had vanished.

❖

The Harpers were, of course, badly affected by all the strange happenings. From the start, the spirits had focused their efforts on Janet, and the longer the haunting continued, the more harm they seemed to be doing her. First, her schoolwork began to suffer, and then her personality started to change. Playfair began to worry that she might even have become possessed by spirits. Fearing for her health, he arranged for her to spend some time in the Maudsley Hospital in London, which specializes in psychiatric illnesses. Away from the house, she seemed to make a full recovery, and after three months she was well enough to leave the hospital.

During Janet's stay in the Maudsley, odd events continued to happen in the Harper's house – chairs flipped over, and doors opened and closed of their own accord – but Janet's time in hospital seemed to mark the beginning of the end of the haunting. When she came home, the family were still subjected to odd incidents. But these were slight compared to the previous ones, and the family shrugged them off as mere inconveniences. Then, shortly after Janet returned, the family was rehoused, and the haunting ceased abruptly.

Afterwards

There was to be a strange footnote to the case of "The House of Strange Happenings". Soon after Janet returned home, a Dutch journalist came to visit the house. He brought with him another medium, a young man named Dono Gmelig-Meyling. Like all the other mediums who had visited, Gmelig-Meyling was sure he was in the presence of a supernatural being. But the ghost he was aware of had nothing in common with any of the previously described spirits. Gmelig-Meyling talked of a 24-year-old woman. Curiously, he mentioned that this spirit had a strong connection with Maurice Grosse.

Grosse was intrigued, and revealed that his daughter had been killed in a motorcycle accident just a couple of weeks before the disturbances at Enfield began. At the time of his first visit she would have been 24. It was enough to convince the medium. "I'm sure it's your daughter," he said.

Grosse and Playfair decided that the dead daughter had not been directly responsible for the hauntings, but that she had used the events in Enfield as a way of contacting her father. For more than a year, Grosse had spent much of his time in the house, and had often wondered why it held such a strong fascination for him. The medium's suggestion seemed to provide an answer.

The Faces on the Floor

For Maria Gomez Pereira, it was just another morning in August 1971. Life in the small Andalusian village of Belmez de la Moraleda was as predictable as the seasons. But when Maria ambled from her bed and into the kitchen of the small house she shared with her sheep-herding husband and their children, she saw something that would change her life forever.

There on the concrete floor was the outline of what looked like a human face. At first Maria thought it must be a shape created by water getting into the floor, and paid it little attention. But over the week the image grew clearer, and she and her husband, Juan Pereira Sanchez, began to point it out to friends who came to visit. Word of this strange discovery quickly spread through the village, and soon Maria and Juan were plagued by a regular stream of curious visitors.

❖

The family found the face's sudden appearance disturbing, and the attention they were getting was beginning to bother them. The couple's son Miguel thought he had a foolproof solution: he took a sledge hammer to the concrete floor and smashed the face to pieces. Then he cemented over the damaged area.

But Miguel's hasty and drastic actions were wasted. A week later another face began to appear in exactly the same spot. At first, only the eyes could be seen. Then a nose appeared, followed by lips and a chin. Before long a portrait of an unknown man stood staring up at them from the floor.

News of this latest mystery spread throughout the village and further afield. Police had to be called out to control crowds who gathered outside the house, all hoping to get a glance of this amazing picture. The story soon reached the ears of local government officials, who decided to investigate the phenomenon more closely.

Orders were given for the piece of kitchen floor concrete to be carefully cut out and sent away for expert analysis. But the scientists who examined it could find nothing to suggest how the picture had been made. The strange face was duly returned to the family. They had it mounted behind a piece of glass and hung it by their fireplace as a memento of their bizarre experience.

Still, the workers who had dug the concrete from the floor had made one eerie discovery. After the top layer of concrete had been removed, they had dug down further. Around 3m (10ft) below the floor they had come across human bones. This came as no surprise to some local people, who recalled that the street had been built on the site of an ancient cemetery. But, even if this offered some vague connection, why should Maria and Juan be singled out, rather than anyone else in the street?

Meanwhile, the floor was relaid, and normality returned to Belmez de la Moraleda. But not for long. Around two weeks later, a third face began to appear on the floor. Once again Miguel's patience snapped. He had had enough of all the intrusions, digging and tinkering, and he smashed it to pieces. Again, his efforts were in vain. No sooner had a fresh layer of new cement settled and set than another face began to appear. This time the face was female, and a dozen or so smaller faces began to appear around it.

Shortly after this, Juan died. Perhaps the strain and intrusion brought about his demise, but the arrival of the faces was not enough to drive Maria away from her family home. As time went by she watched them come and go. Some stayed on the floor for six months or more, before disappearing just as mysteriously as they had arrived. Others came and went within a single day.

Sometimes Maria tried to scrub the faces off the floor when they started to appear, but her efforts here were fruitless. But she did notice that cutting the faces out of the floor seemed to freeze their development: the features stopped altering, which they were constantly doing when the floor remained in place.

❖

Over the years, a steady stream of investigators came to the house. Despite the Pereiras obvious irritation with all the attention they were getting, many investigators suspected Maria and her family were faking the phenomenon for reasons of their own. Some suggested that someone must be sneaking into the kitchen when no one was in the house, and drawing on the floor.

One team of paranormal investigators went to extraordinary lengths to rule out the possibility of faking. They sealed off the kitchen and covered its floor from wall to wall with clear plastic sheeting. Then they rigged up remote control cameras, planning to take photographs at regular intervals to see if any new faces developed.

But the experiment had several important flaws.

There wasn't enough light for the photographs to come out, but when they used lamps to light the kitchen, the glare of the bulbs on the plastic stopped anything on the floor from showing up on the film. Eventually, wet patches started forming beneath the plastic sheeting, which had to be removed. The experiment had been a total failure.

Other sceptical investigators came up with a string of suggestions to explain the appearance of the faces. They said that someone had been using soot and vinegar, or a chemical product, to remove stains from concrete. But scientists were unable to find any evidence that these substances had been used, and no one was ever caught drawing on the floor.

❖

In all their time investigating the strange phenomena at Belmez de la Moraleda, observers only witnessed faces forming on the floor on two occasions. A doctor was setting up his camera to photograph the kitchen when he noticed a small grey cloud appearing on the floor. When it cleared, new details of a face could be seen. On another occasion, several people together in the room witnessed the same thing happening.

The faces at Belmez de la Moraleda were not particularly sinister. The family of Maria and Juan had no dark secrets or bloody feuds. No one ever offered a convincing explanation as to why the faces appeared, and no one has been able to prove the phenomenon was faked. Some things, it seems, are beyond rational scientific explanation.

Afterwards

Belmez de la Moraleda is now a standard tourist stop for coach parties from the Costa del Sol – Spain's famous tourist region. Fresh pictures still appear and disappear and, at the time of writing, Maria Gomez Pereira still lives in her little house.

The Most Haunted House in England

Deep in the English countryside, huddled between the windswept Essex coast and flat lowlands of Suffolk, lies the lonely village of Borley. Set in its heart, among drab cottages and tattered oaks, is an ancient parish church. It was here that the Reverend Henry Bull arrived in 1862 to take up his appointment as parson to the village. Windswept and lonely it may have been, but Bull liked his parish. In fact, he liked it so much that he decided to build a new rectory to accommodate his large family of 14 children.

The locals felt he could have chosen a more appropriate site. There was much gossip about the land around the church being haunted, and reports of shadowy figures being seen lurking in the area. Borley's new rectory was built on the very spot where an old mansion had once stood. That mansion, in turn, had been built on the site of an ancient monastery. The monastery had had a sinister reputation. It was said that a young novice nun from a convent nearby had had a love affair with a monk from the monastery. The couple had decided to run away, but were discovered as they were leaving together. As their punishment, they were both condemned to death. The monk was hanged, but the poor nun faced a much more cruel fate. She was bricked up in a wall alive, and left to die inside it.

Henry Bull was not the sort of man to be put off by a few ghost stories. His magnificent new residence was a huge rambling place boasting 35 rooms. But it also had a dingy attic and a damp cellar, which was soon infested with frogs and toads.

Right from the start, the Bull family was subjected to a series of strange happenings. One of Bull's daughters, in particular, regularly heard footsteps outside her room at night. The steps would stop, and then something would tap three times on her door. Always three times, and always there would be no one there.

Bull himself claimed to have seen several different ghosts, including a pair of phantom legs disappearing through a gate. But the most persistent apparition was a nun whom he would occasionally glimpse in the garden. Bull enjoyed seeing these ghosts. He even built a summerhouse at the end of the garden where he would sit and smoke a cigar, waiting for the nun to appear.

❖

Henry Bull died in 1892, and his son Harry succeeded him at the rectory. His family, too, continued to be visited by ghosts. July 28, 1900 was a particularly memorable day for the Bulls. It was a mild summer evening and three of Harry's sisters were returning from a friend's garden party. They were laughing gaily in the soft, fading light, when they stopped dead in their tracks. There on the rectory lawn was a female figure, draped in a black habit, gliding mysteriously across the front of the house. The sisters had grown up with these strange happenings. They were more curious than frightened, and this particular apparition seemed particularly vivid. One of the girls stepped forward boldly, intending to talk to the figure, but the ghost simply vanished before their eyes.

The family was also disturbed by the sound of a rattling coach passing down the lane next to the house. Harry would stand outside, waiting to catch sight of the vehicle, but the rattling would always fade away before the coach could be seen. Harry Bull never did see the coach, but other members of the Borley Rectory household did — especially the gardener. On one moonlit night he watched it for 30 seconds as it swept through trees, walls and hedges, before vanishing into a nearby farmyard.

❖

Harry Bull died in 1927 and Borley Rectory stood empty for a year until the arrival of a new vicar, Eric Smith. He and his wife didn't believe in ghosts, but even they couldn't deny that the house was troubled by strange goings-on. Smith heard inexplicable whisperings, footsteps and bells ringing. Two of his maids reported seeing the nun, and one saw the coach thunder by. She was also terrified by the sight of a headless man.

The Smiths were subjected to a new and unnerving form of ghostly activity which had never troubled the Bulls. Now keys would shoot out of locks, and dishes would tumble down from the table without warning. The Smiths were beginning to feel most unwelcome at Borley, and their once confident dismissal of ghosts and hauntings was replaced by a baffled concern.

In desperation Eric Smith wrote to a national newspaper, the *Daily Mirror*, in the hope of contacting an investigator. The paper sent him Harry Price — the best-known ghost hunter of his day. Right from the start, Price was to be rewarded with a series of extraordinary manifestations of supernatural power.

On his first visit to Borley, Price and a *Mirror* reporter were showered with breaking glass as they entered the rectory's front door. A brick had fallen onto a glass awning above the door. That evening, Borley's residents were treated to a spectacular display of poltergeist activity. A glass candlestick flew down the stairs and shattered on the hall floor below. In the dining room, keys in two doors shot out of locks at the same time. In the bathroom, a bar of soap jumped into the air.

It was all very exciting, and Price and the reporter duly wrote sensational accounts of their stay for the *Daily Mirror*. Almost overnight, the publicity turned Borley Rectory into a tourist attraction. Coach trips were even organized to visit the "haunted house".

Eric Smith bitterly regretted the day he had written to the *Daily Mirror*. Thanks to this unwanted attention, his dream of a quiet life was in ruins. He and his wife moved out, leaving the rectory to an eerie silence.

❖

It was to be another year before the parish was provided with a new vicar. His name was the Reverend Lionel Foyster – a cousin of Harry Bull's. He brought with him his young wife, Marianne, and their family to live at the rectory. Unlike Eric Smith, Foyster did believe in ghosts, and was intrigued by the stories he had heard about his new house. Right from the start he kept a journal, where he recorded every odd incident – from objects disappearing, to bells ringing, and furniture overturning.

But with the arrival of the Foysters, the haunting of Borley Rectory took on a sinister new twist. The ghostly manifestations became more violent, and seemed to be focused specifically on Marianne. She would be thrown from her bed, and struck by an unseen hand. Most disturbing of all, mysterious writing would appear on the walls, begging for help.

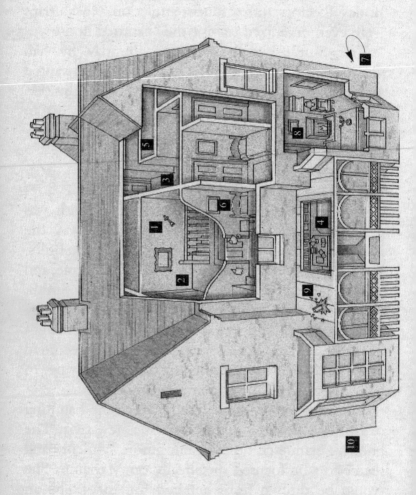

The Most Haunted House in England

The locations of some of the ghostly sightings and poltergeist activity at Borley

1. **Main staircase**. Site of many ghostly footsteps. On one occasion a glass candlestick flew down the stairs.

2. **First floor landing**. The "cold spot". Tests showed this spot was sometimes several degrees colder than the surrounding area.

3. **Landing** to rear of the house. Most of the written messages to Marianne Foyster appeared here.

4. **Study**. Harry Price's base for investigations. Once, an invisible presence locked the door from the inside, while Price was in the room.

5. **Bathroom**. One resident was attacked by a poltergeist outside the bathroom door.

6. **Front bedroom**. Known as the "Blue Room", after its paint scheme, this was the most haunted part of the house. Strange forces threw people out of bed, or levitated ornaments.

7. **Kitchen**. Dishes were thrown around here by invisible forces. Bells for summoning servants continued to ring, even though they had been disconnected.

8. **Dining room**. The phantom nun was often seen staring though the window. The Bulls had the window blocked up.

9. **Veranda**. When Harry Price first arrived, a brick shattered the glass roof, showering him with glass.

10. **Garden**. Scene of many hauntings, including those by the ghostly nun and the phantom coach.

Written in a childish hand, it would say "Marianne, please help…", or other plaintive pleas. On one occasion, Marianne saw the words forming on the wall, and asked the spirit what it wanted; "Rest…" came the distressing reply. From certain phrases the spirit used, Marianne guessed the words were coming from a young Catholic woman.

Other odd incidents continued to happen, and the Reverend Foyster recorded over 2,000 of them in his journal. Marianne, though, found the constant ghostly presence too much to bear. She began spending weekdays in London, only returning to Borley at the weekend. Curiously, the rate of supernatural activity dropped sharply when she was not in the house. Price, who was still following the haunting, even came to the conclusion that Marianne had faked many of the events. But even so, that would still not explain all of them.

❖

Like the Smiths before them, the Foysters could only take so much. After a harrowing five years, they moved out of the rectory. A new vicar was appointed to the parish, but he arranged to live elsewhere. Clearly, the rectory had become anything but a place of comfort and refuge.

For 18 months the haunted house lay empty. Then Harry Price decided he would rent it for a year. He had no intention of living there, but wanted to bring in teams of observers to gather further evidence. To recruit them, he placed an advert in what was one of Britain's most respectable newspapers – *The Times* – and received hundreds of replies.

Price chose 48 of what he called "the right sort of people": doctors, engineers, scientists and army officers. They were professionals whose reputation depended on integrity and honesty, whom Price felt he could trust. These people stayed in the house for a few days at a time, and were provided with a set of instructions. Other than that, they were left to their own devices.

The results of this ambitious experiment were mainly disappointing. Volunteers reported many incidents, but they were mostly insubstantial – lights might flicker on, or they would hear the odd noise, or witness occasional slight movements of furniture. What was intriguing, though, were the results of one volunteer's experiments with a planchette – a heart-shaped board set on wheels. With this device, a pencil is placed in the middle of the board with its tip pointing down. The idea is that someone sits with their hand flat on the planchette. Then it moves of its own accord, guided by an unknown presence, spelling out messages from the spirit world.

The planchette's message was a chilling one. It told the tale of a French nun named Marie Lairre, who had been taken from a nearby convent by a local landowner, and strangled. As the planchette spelled out its story, it even gave an exact date – May 17,

1667. Could this be the ghostly nun, Price wondered? Another session with the planchette produced a sensational prediction: Borley Rectory would burn down that very night. It also claimed that the bones of the murdered nun would be found buried beneath the charred ruins, under the brick floor of the cellar.

❖

The rectory did not burn down that night, and Harry Price's year-long lease came to an end. The mystery of Borley Rectory was still unsolved. The house, now deemed unsuitable for a church property, was put up for sale. It was bought by a man named Captain Gregson in 1939.

While Gregson was unpacking his belongings, a lit oil lamp in the hall overturned. It shattered on the hard floor, and a sheet of flame quickly spread to the carpets and curtains. Gregson escaped, but fire consumed the house and, by the next morning, Borley rectory was a smoking, burned-out shell. The planchette's timing may have been wrong, but its prediction had come eerily true.

Price soon found out what had happened, and was anxious to follow up the second half of the planchette's claim – that the bones of the nun would be found in the ruins. But, at this time, Britain was embroiled in the Second World War, and an invasion by Nazi Germany seemed imminent. Clearly, there were more important things on people's minds. By 1943, however, although the war was still being waged, the tide had begun to turn against Germany. Now Price approached Captain Gregson and asked for his permission to excavate the ruins.

Price hired a crew of men to dig through the ruins, and they soon cleared a path down to the cellar. Then, according to the instructions of the planchette, they started digging under the bricks which lined the cellar floor.

Within a day, Price and his crew had unearthed several fragile fragments of a skeleton – a jawbone and part of a skull. These were examined by forensic scientists. The scientists declared that the bone fragments belonged to a woman aged about 30. Price was sure they were the remains of Marie Lairre. In 1945, he arranged for them to be given a Christian burial in nearby Borley churchyard.

The remains of the ill-fated rectory were demolished in 1944, but the hauntings were not yet at an end. In 1949, a local doctor was startled to see the figure of a nun near the old rectory gates. It vanished mysteriously as he approached. A family living nearby also claimed to have seen a similar apparition.

New houses now stand where the rectory garden used to be. It is said that sightings of the nun still continue. Burial of her bones in hallowed ground, it seems, was not enough to drive away her restless spirit.

Afterwards

The haunting of Borley Rectory continues to perplex students of the supernatural. Its principal investigator, Harry Price, died in 1948, but not before he had written two sensational books on the subject, which became best sellers. Seven years after his death, three other psychic researchers produced their own report on Borley, claiming that Price had faked much of the haunting himself.

One example they cited as evidence was an incident where a reporter had witnessed pebbles flying around the house at night. Not easily frightened, the reporter had grabbed hold of Harry Price only to find his pockets were full of pebbles.

The researchers concluded that Price had slanted evidence in order to make sensational reading for the public. He certainly had a strong motive for doing so – his whole career was built around his reputation as a ghost hunter.

Marianne Foyster was also interviewed when she was in her late 70s. She admitted that many of the events were of her own making. She used the hauntings as an excuse to spend time away from the dreary village in the bright lights of London. She did, though, continue to insist that strange things had happened at Borley which had had nothing to do with her.

Perhaps the poltergeist aspects of the haunting – with objects flying through the air – were all faked.

They increased dramatically with the arrival of Price and reached even higher levels when Marianne moved in. But, despite this, so many other incidents have no natural explanation that it seems Borley Rectory still deserves its title of the most haunted house in England.

The Jinx on UB-65

Admiral Schroeder, the head of the German U-boat submarine fleet during the First World War, knew that it was time for drastic action. He had just discovered that submarine UB-65 was plagued by crew members asking for transfers to other submarines. Why? Because they believed their boat was haunted.

"*Haunted*?" Schroeder snorted with indignation, as he sat glancing over the official UB-65 report, marked "Top Secret", in his War Department office. "This is the *20th century*, for Heaven's sake".

In early 1918, Germany needed every U-boat she could muster, and there was nothing wrong with UB-65. Except that it was "haunted".

Schroeder called his adjutant over from the next office. "Make arrangements for me at once, to travel to Wilhelmshaven. I shall be spending the night aboard this so-called 'haunted' submarine."

"Yes, Herr Admiral," snapped the adjutant, saluting smartly.

The very next day Schroeder took a staff car to the submarine fleet headquarters at Wilhelmshaven, and went at once to the troubled vessel.

Piped aboard with maximum pomp and ceremony, Schroeder summoned the crew and told them he had never heard such an extraordinary story in his life. But to show them that he was a reasonable man who understood their fears, he would spend the night, alone, in the submarine, to see if there was any substance to the stories.

And so he did.

❖

The crew members were all summoned from shore barracks the next morning, and stood on parade before their boat. Admiral Schroeder emerged from the conning tower looking bright and breezy.

"Gentlemen," he announced, "I have to tell you I have rarely slept better in my life. This fine vessel is in peak condition, and it is desperately needed to defend the Fatherland. I have every confidence that you will set sail, safe and unhindered, on your forthcoming mission. Let there be no more talk of ghosts and hauntings."

The crew stood stiffly at attention, and the Admiral disappeared into his car and left. However, Schroeder's common-sense approach might have had more effect on the men if someone else at the port had not arranged for a priest to carry out an exorcism later that day. And besides, if UB-65 was haunted, its phantoms were far too cunning to put in an appearance at a time like this. They liked to torment their victims out in the lonely ocean, far away from shore and safety.

❖

Admiral Schroeder might have been a little more sympathetic if he had taken the trouble to find out more about the troubled submarine. UB-65 did indeed have a distressing history. She had been built in early 1916, and right from the start things seemed to go wrong. A week after construction began, a heavy steel girder fell from an overhead crane, crushing two workers to death. Then, when the engine was being fitted, three more workers were overcome with fumes and died.

Things got no better after the submarine was launched. On a trial run out to sea, a crew member was swept overboard and drowned. Then, on UB-65's first underwater test, the boat developed a serious leak which stopped it from resurfacing. For nearly 12 agonizing hours, the submarine was stuck under water. The crew fought for their lives, and when the boat finally surfaced, they struggled from the entry hatches gasping for air, and all convinced that their craft was fatally jinxed.

The officers tried hard to put a stop to such defeatist talk, but the very next day, things got even worse. As the torpedoes were being loaded in preparation for the submarine's first mission of the war, one of them exploded. Five seamen were killed, including the craft's second-in-command, Lieutenant Richter.

Replacements were drafted in and the crew continued to prepare for their first mission out to sea. The day of their departure was marred by another incident. As the captain, Lieutenant Commander Gustav Schelle, stood discussing their route with the submarine's chief navigator, a terrified seaman ran up to him and stammered out an unlikely story.

"Herr Captain, I have just seen Lieutenant Richter come on board. He walked to the bow, and then turned toward the conning tower, and stood there, as he used to do, with his arms folded."

"You're drunk, man," thundered Schelle angrily.

"Oh no, sir," said the seaman recovering his composure. "Furthermore, Gunner Petersen also saw our Lieutenant."

The captain and two other officers immediately went to look for Petersen. They found him soon enough, on the lower deck of the submarine. He was squatting on his haunches, curled up in terror. Schelle immediately sent for the Wilhelmshaven chaplain, who spent an hour talking to the man. But his efforts were wasted. Just before UB-65 set sail, Petersen deserted, and was never seen again. Morale slumped, and the nervous crew members wondered what fate had in store for their first wartime voyage.

As it turned out, they needn't have worried. The mission was a great success. In the two months they spent at sea, they sank three enemy ships, and seriously damaged a fourth – all with no casualties to themselves. But there was one sinister incident that impressed the members of the crew far more than any of their military triumphs. It came three weeks into the mission, when the boat was on patrol in the English Channel.

The weather was rough at the time, and heavy seas were breaking over the vessel. Suddenly, the starboard lookout noticed a figure dressed in an officer's overcoat, standing alone on the deck among the breakers.

The watchman rubbed his eyes in disbelief, for he knew all the ship's hatches had been fastened tight to prevent the waves from swamping the boat. How could it be, that this man had gone out on the deck, and was not being washed overboard? But then the figure turned toward him, and the watchman recognized him at once. It was Lieutenant Richter, four weeks dead, and buried at the seamen's cemetery at Wilhelmshaven.

❖

Its time at sea over, UB-65 returned to base for a routine refit and resupply. Richter's supposed appearance was duly reported, and the submarine was closely examined for leaking fumes that might have caused the crew to hallucinate. But nothing unusual was found.

It was then that crew members started to request transfers *en masse*, and word of the ship's troubles reached Admiral Schroeder. Following the Admiral's visit, Captain Schelle did everything he could to discourage talk of ghosts. He let it be known that anyone who reported seeing a ghost would be severely punished. At first, his threat worked. Whatever his men whispered to each other in private, there was no more public mention of anything supernatural for some months.

But tension aboard the vessel began to mount. Even at the best of times, submarines were difficult places to live. They were cramped, hot and foul-smelling, with living accommodation squeezed into crannies wherever the equipment allowed. Beds were stacked in tiers close to live torpedoes, and the seamen didn't even own their own bunks. They shared them, still warm from the previous occupant, in eight-hour shifts.

As the war dragged on, and one patrol succeeded another, the strain on the sailors' nerves increased. German U-boat losses were mounting, and the men knew they had only a 50-50 chance of getting home again. Even in the best of submarines, the sailors began to call their vessels "steel coffins".

Nowhere was this grim anxiety more keenly felt than on UB-65. In May 1918, a gunner on the submarine went berserk. He rushed into the control room shouting that he had just seen Lieutenant Richter standing by the bow torpedo tubes. He was so hysterical that he had to be given drugs to calm him down. A few hours later, he seemed normal again. He was allowed out of his bunk, and told to report back to his station aboard the submarine. This proved to be a mistake. A little later, he walked out onto the deck of the vessel and threw himself overboard.

His death seemed to trigger a new wave of troubles. A week later, one of the ship's officers was swept overboard. Then, the chief engineer broke his leg as he ran down one of UB-65's steep steel ladders. Not long after this, the submarine dived too deeply, while trying to escape from an enemy submarine. The boat had to surface again quickly, and only narrowly escaped detection.

On another occasion soon after, the submarine was attacked by an enemy patrol. Depth charges (explosives, launched from ships, which explode underwater) rained down on UB-65 for more than an hour. The shock waves threw one man to the ground with such force that he was badly hurt and later died of his injuries.

❖

Nonetheless, UB-65 survived this mission, and returned to port to refuel and take on fresh supplies. The war was coming to a climax, and she was dispatched to sea again almost immediately, with barely a moment's rest for her jittery, anxious crew. It was to be their last voyage.

UB-65's final appearance became one of World War One's most intriguing mysteries. Around 6:30 on the evening of July 10, 1918, an American submarine was cruising off the south coast of Ireland. Its commander, Lieutenant Forster, noticed what he thought was a buoy, floating on the horizon. Moving cautiously closer to examine this item, he realized it was actually a German submarine, later identified from official records as UB-65. It was listing heavily in the water, and seemed to have been badly damaged.

Lieutenant Forster was immediately fearful of a trap, thinking that UB-65 had been left to drift on the surface as a lure. He thought the best course of action was to sink it quickly, and then leave the area immediately. But as he guided his craft carefully around it, hoping to line up a torpedo shot, UB-65 was torn apart by a huge explosion which sent metal fragments and spray flying high into the air. Then, the submarine rose up on its bows, and sank to the bottom of the Atlantic. There were no survivors, and no bodies were ever recovered.

Afterwards

The explosion has never been satisfactorily explained. Perhaps Forster was right to expect a trap. Maybe there was another German submarine circling close by, and UB-65 had been blown up by a torpedo aimed at the American vessel?

But there is another mystery. According to one source, Lieutenant Forster thought he saw someone on deck, just before UB-65 exploded. It was a figure in a German officer's overcoat, standing near to the bow with folded arms. If this can be believed, perhaps it was Lieutenant Richter putting in a final appearance?

The Bell Witch

Those who see them may be filled with dread, but, according to witnesses' accounts, ghosts rarely do anyone any actual harm. Even when poltergeists throw objects across the room, they rarely hit their human targets with any great force. But one famous haunting in Tennessee, in the early 19th century, was to have fatal consequences for its victims – the Bell family of Robertson County.

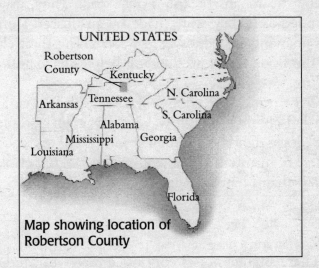

Map showing location of Robertson County

In 1817 John Bell was a prosperous cotton farmer. The plantation he owned, like all of those in the

79

southern states of America at the time, was worked largely by slaves. Yet Bell does not seem to have been a particularly harsh master. He, his wife Lucy and their nine children were devout Christians, and open cruelty to the slaves would not have fitted well with their religious beliefs. It is almost certain that none of Bell's slaves had a hand in the events that followed.

But, during this year, strange happenings began to occur in the Bell household. At first, these incidents seemed harmless enough. Tappings and scrapings were heard on the doors and windows at night. Yet, whenever the family lit lamps and went to investigate, the sounds would stop. Then noises began to be heard inside the house too. They usually sounded as if they were made by an unseen animal: rats gnawing at bedposts, dogs scratching their claws on the floor, or a bird flapping helplessly against the ceiling.

Over time, the noises became more violent. Startled children would wake to hear what sounded like dogs fighting in their rooms. There was the clatter of furniture being overturned and the clank of heavy chains being dragged across the floor.

❖

These strange noises continued for a year, and the Bell family became increasingly uneasy. Then, suddenly, things got worse. Whatever was bothering them began to make its presence felt in more physical ways. It started to pull the bedclothes from sleeping children. A guest who was staying at the house was woken in this way. Seeing the blankets wrapped around what looked like a human form he seized the bundle, shouting: "I have the ghost!" Grasping it tightly, the man headed for the still burning fire, intending to throw it in, and rid the house of its phantom tormentor forever.

But, before he could reach the fireplace, the room was filled with an overpowering stink. The smell was so awful, the man began to retch. Feeling he was about to be sick, he immediately dropped the blankets and headed outside for fresher air. When he returned to the room, the stench was gone, and so was the ghost.

On another occasion, John Bell's son, Richard, woke up screaming. His hair was being pulled so hard he thought the top of his scalp was going to be torn off. As his parents rushed to help him, they were distracted by cries coming from another bedroom. Exactly the same thing was happening to his elder sister, Betsy.

Along with the attacks, the ghost had begun to make a bizarre variety of almost human sounds. There would be gulping, lip smacking, and a particularly horrible choking gurgle, which sounded like someone being strangled.

For John and Lucy Bell, the attacks on the children were the last straw. Until then, they had kept quiet about the haunting, fearing no one would believe them. Now, they turned to a close friend named James Johnson for assistance.

Johnson was intrigued by what he heard, and very much wanted to talk to this strange, unwanted visitor. So, whenever it made its presence felt in the Bell household, he would go there and ask questions. At first, the only answer he got was a faint whistling. Then, after several days, there was a feeble whispering, too quiet to understand. Before long though, the volume increased, and the words were coming through loud and clear.

This voice seemed to draw its power from Betsy, who was now a teenager, and increasingly the focus for the hauntings. The ghost rarely put in an appearance when she wasn't around. The haunting made her anxious and unhappy, but it also began to affect her physically too. She started suffering from giddy spells in which she became abruptly short of breath.

Sometimes, she would fall into a trance for 30 or 40 minutes. Then, when she came back to consciousness, the ghost would start talking, almost as if it needed to draw energy from her before it could make itself heard.

Some visitors to the house who witnessed these extraordinary manifestations suspected that Betsy was playing a game, and using ventriloquism to create the voices around the house. A doctor was called to test out this theory. As the ghost spoke, the doctor placed his hand over Betsy's vocal chords. He insisted he could feel no movement there, and was convinced Betsy had no part in creating the sounds.

Now that the ghost could speak, James Johnson and the Bells could ask it questions. But the most obvious one – who was it? – produced a string of contradictory replies. Early on, it stated: "I am a spirit who was once very happy, but have been disturbed and am now unhappy." Later, it claimed to be an American Indian whose bones had been disturbed. Then it claimed be a local woman named Kate Batt, who had been accused of being a witch.

Before too long, a whole host of different voices were making themselves heard. They called themselves by unusual names, such as Blackdog and Jerusalem, and described themselves as "the family of Kate Batt". By that, Johnson and the Bells took it to mean that Kate Batt had summoned a host of spirits in a witchcraft ritual, and they were now dealing with the consequences of her occult tampering. But Kate Batt was now long gone, driven from Robertson County by an angry mob. She had fled north, to who knows where.

❖

The mystery remained unsolved, and the Bells just got on with their lives as best they could. The Bell Witch, as it was now known, seemed to have a variety of different personalities – perhaps unsurprisingly, considering how many people it said it was. Some of these personalities were friendly, while others most definitely were not.

The witch could be particularly helpful to members of the family it liked. On one occasion, it was even said to have saved the life of one of the Bell boys. He became caught in quicksand while crawling though a narrow passage in a cave near to the house. Suddenly, the cave was lit up and an unearthly voice called: "I'll get you out!" The next thing the boy knew was that his legs had been seized by what felt like strong hands, and he was pulled to safety.

The witch seemed to have a particular soft spot for Lucy Bell. It became an invisible presence at the Bible study groups she organized. Here, it displayed a hitherto unseen talent. When the group decided to take a break, fruit would materialize from nowhere, and drop into the laps of the astonished guests. What they made of this unnatural phenomenon is not recorded.

On one occasion, when Lucy fell ill, the ghost was heard whispering: "Luce, poor Luce, how do you feel now?" Then, the ailing woman was showered with hazelnuts. Perhaps Lucy Bell was dreaming, or having a fevered hallucination, but, when she recovered, she was sure the ghost had paid her a friendly visit.

When the ghost was showing its more malevolent side, it victimized Betsy Bell. It frequently pulled her hair or slapped her face. Sometimes, visitors to the house would also feel a stinging blow to their faces or arms, and later find a red mark on their bodies where the blow had struck home.

Betsy grew increasingly fearful of these attacks, which would occur without rhyme or reason. At one point she was sent to live at a friend's house nearby, in the hope that this would bring the disturbances to a halt. However, the move made little difference. Noises were still heard in the Bell house, and Betsy continued to be slapped.

❖

The years passed and Betsy, now 16, was engaged to be married. The ghost's vendetta against her grew more intense. Often, when Betsy and her fiancé, Joshua Gardner, were in company, the phantom voice would make crude or offensive remarks about them. Betsy would sometimes grow so embarrassed that she would run screaming from the room. At other times, as she lay alone in her bed at night, she would hear a pleading voice repeating, over and over: "Please, Betsy Bell, don't have Joshua Gardner." The strain became too much for her. Eventually, Betsy broke off the engagement.

Yet there was worse to come. Much worse. The ghost's next target was the head of the family, "Old Jack Bell", as the witch had taken to calling him. From early on in the haunting, John Bell had complained of stiffness in the mouth; it felt, he said, as though someone were pushing a stick sideways into it, forcing his jaws apart. Now his tongue became so swollen that whole days would pass when he could not eat or speak. He developed spasms and twitches that would contort his face horribly.

By December 1820, John Bell was a very sick man. He took to his bed for a week, during which time the witch tormented him continually. Eventually, he got up to go for a walk with his son Richard. But, outside the house, John was stopped in his tracks by a stunning blow to the cheek. He sat down on a log to catch his breath. Then his face started convulsing, and his shoes flew off. Richard knelt down to put them back on, but every time he did so they would fly off again. John Bell sat on a log in his garden with tears rolling down his face, crying like a helpless child tormented by a playground bully. All the while, the ghost howled and shrieked with malicious glee.

The end came just before Christmas. On the morning of December 20, John Bell seemed sound asleep, but after breakfast his family realized he had fallen into a coma. His son, John Junior, went to a cupboard where his medicine was kept. He made an alarming discovery. The medicine the family doctor had given him was gone. In its place was a smoky-looking flask, one-third full of a dark liquid. A servant was sent to summon the doctor, while the voice of the witch reverberated around the house.

"I've got him this time," it chuckled. "He'll never get up from that bed again."

The doctor arrived and decided to test the

contents of the flask on the family cat. Perhaps he should have tried the suspicious-looking liquid on a less well-loved animal. The cat tasted it, gave a sudden leap, whirled around three times, then fell dead. Surprisingly, rather than handing the flask over to the local sheriff, the doctor immediately poured the rest of the liquid onto the fire, where it could do no more harm. Perhaps he was so caught up in the story of the haunting that it did not occur to him someone might be trying to murder John Bell by poisoning him. If this was the case, then the doctor had just destroyed some vital evidence.

The next morning, Bell was pronounced dead. Even at his funeral, the ghost did not leave him alone. Bizarre shrieks of rejoicing were heard during the service, and the ceremony was disrupted by a voice singing a Tennessee drinking song.

❖

The hauntings continued for some months after John Bell's death, but nothing quite so dramatic would happen again. Then, one night in the spring of 1821, the family were relaxing after dinner when they heard a noise of something heavy, like a cannon ball, falling down the chimney. A black ball crashed into the hearth, and rolled out onto the grate, where it exploded in a puff of smoke. Then a familiar voice called out in a shrill, peevish manner: "I'm going, and will be gone for seven years. Goodbye."

And that was that. The Bells enjoyed seven years of peace, and the Bell Witch haunting became a slowly receding bad memory. When the time came for the witch to return, only Lucy and two of her sons were still living at home. Their hearts sank when the knocking began again, and bedclothes were pulled back as before. But, this time, the family agreed to ignore the witch, and after two weeks it stopped visiting them. There was evidently little fun in tormenting people who showed no annoyance or fear.

The ghost moved on to John Bell Junior's new home. Here it announced to Bell's startled family that it would return in 107 years. That was in 1828. If anything strange happened in the house in 1935, it went unrecorded.

Afterwards

Almost two centuries on, the Bell Witch affair remains an unsolved mystery. Over the first four years of the haunting, which ended in John Bell's death, the strange events at the house were witnessed by both family members and dozens of outside visitors.

John Bell's son Richard wrote about the ghost in his book, *Our Family Trouble*, published in 1846, 25 years after the events it describes.

The Tennessee haunting has been described as "the greatest American ghost story", but the possibility exists that it was really a cleverly planned murder. John Bell's death was almost certainly not due to natural causes, yet no one was ever taken to court over this. Did Bell really fall victim to supernatural forces, or was he killed by human hands? Either way, the story of his death must rank as one of the world's strangest unsolved murders.

The Restless Tomb

'As quiet as the grave' was a saying that could never be applied to the Chase family vault in Barbados. For here, it seemed, bodies lay uneasy in their coffins. The mystery that overtook the peaceful cemetery at Christchurch, near the West Indian island's southern tip, began in the early 19th century.

The vault was originally built in the 1720s, but apparently it was still lying empty in 1807, when the body of a Mrs. Thomasina Goddard was buried there in a wooden coffin. Shortly after this, the vault came into the possession of the Chase family, and three of its members were interred there over the next five years. The first was a two-year-old girl named Mary Anne Chase, who died in February, 1808. Four years later, she was joined by her elder sister, Dorcas.

Nothing strange was noticed at the time of these early burials, and in those days it was common for children to die so young. But a mere 34 days after Dorcas was laid to rest, her father, the Honourable Thomas Chase, died too. When he was buried, the workers who carried his coffin into the vault found that the two coffins belonging to Mary Anne and Dorcas had been moved. Mary Anne's, in fact, looked as if it had been hurled from one corner of the vault to the other, where it had come to rest head down. The workers were disturbed by what they saw. But they dutifully set the coffins back in place, and then brought in the coffin of Thomas Chase and laid it down beside them. They also told the Christchurch vicar what they had seen.

❖

It was four years before the vault was opened again. This time, a Chase family friend, Samuel Brewster, and then his son, were both buried there, two months apart. Each time the vault was opened, cemetery workers found that the coffins had been disturbed. By now, the mystery of the moving coffins was the talking point of Barbados. So, when the vault was opened again three years later, the British governor of Barbados, Lord Combermere, decided to see for himself. He was not disappointed. A crowd gathered to witness the opening of the vault. As soon as the marble slab that covered its entrance was removed, everyone could see that the coffins had shifted once more.

The body due to be interred in the vault was that of a woman named Thomazina Clarke. But before she could be buried, Lord Combermere ordered elaborate precautions to be taken. First, the walls and floor of the vault were "sounded", to make sure there were no secret passages. To do this, cemetery workers

The Restless Tomb

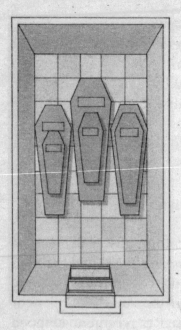

How the coffins were originally placed in the Chase vault

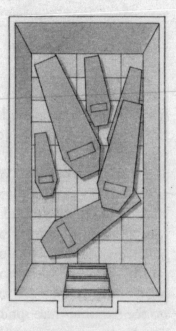

The coffins as they were found when the vault was reopened

went around tapping on all the surfaces to see if a different, more hollow-sounding tap revealed a hidden chamber. Then, when the new coffin had been laid in place, the bearers sprinkled fine sand over the floor so that any footmarks would show up. Finally, the marble slab which closed the tomb was cemented back into place. As an extra precaution,

Lord Combermere and several other witnesses put their seals on the wet cement. Now, even if the slab were to be removed and then cemented back up again, it would still be possible to see that someone had broken into the vault.

❖

Lord Combermere returned to Christchurch some nine months later, on April 18, 1820. Here, his curiosity got the better of him, and he decided to have the tomb reopened. First, he examined the seals he had placed on the drying concrete. They were plainly unbroken. Then, witnessed by the local vicar and several others, he ordered the cement chipped away and the marble slab pulled back.

As daylight intruded upon the darkness of the tomb, a gasp of horror went around the crowd who had gathered to witness the opening. Inside, the coffins were jumbled around the vault, as if they had been caught in the eye of a whirlwind. Yet there were no footprints in the sand. What made this even more extraordinary was that since Mrs. Goddard's burial, all the bodies had been interred in heavy lead coffins. These coffins weighed far too much for anyone to be able to move them single-handedly – especially that of Thomas Chase. He had been a very heavy man, and it had taken eight men to carry his coffin into the vault. This should have made it impossible to hurl around.

And there was something else bizarre about the scene. When the vault had last been opened, cemetery workers had found that the wooden coffin of Thomasina Goddard, now buried for some 13 years, had rotted away. As was the practice when this happened, the men had taken what was left and left it standing against a corner in the vault. It was still standing there, untouched. The unknown force that had hurled heavy lead coffins around, as though they were made of matchwood, had left this fragile bundle completely undisturbed.

The people of Barbados were disturbed and unsettled by these events, none more so than the surviving members of the Chase family. Naturally, they had hoped that their loved ones would rest in peace, and the thought that the dead were restless was terrible — even if it defied all reason. Lord Combermere decided that enough was enough. He ordered all the remaining coffins be removed and reburied elsewhere. The vault was left open and unoccupied, and remains so to this day.

Afterwards

What could have brought about such a strange and unnatural occurrence — was there any possible logical explanation? A few possibilities have been suggested. Perhaps the coffins were shifted by minor earth tremors? This may have been so, but there was no evidence of movement in the cemetery's other vaults. Maybe water seeped into the tomb, flooding to such an extent that the coffins floated? When the water receded, they would have been left scattered higgledy-piggledy around the tomb. This too seems unlikely, as there was no sign of dampness. Besides, the sandy floor remained untouched, and water would have disturbed the flimsy remains of Thomasina Goddard's coffin as well.

Then maybe – just maybe – there is the possibility of a supernatural explanation: that the vault was violently haunted, and that a vengeful phantom hurled the coffins around the vault. Island gossip had it that the Chase family was far from contented. The trouble started with the burial of Dorcas, who was a deeply unhappy girl. In her short life she had argued constantly with her domineering father, and had eventually starved herself to death.

Thomas Chase, who was buried a mere three weeks after Dorcas, was said to have killed himself. Perhaps he committed suicide in a fit of remorse brought on by the death of his daughter. If the stories are to be believed, the spirits of the troubled Chase clan of Christchurch had much to be restless about.

Messengers from Beyond the Grave

Reports of hauntings seem to suggest that ghosts are creatures of habit, who come back to frequent the places they used to know. But a few hauntings are different. Some spirits seem to come back especially to pass on a message to the living. Here are three stories of such messengers from beyond the grave.

The Lady in White

English nobleman Thomas, Lord Lyttelton, was famed throughout London for his wild ways. Friends and acquaintances revelled in tales of his debauchery and wickedness. They reckoned that, if even half of what they heard about him was true, Lord Lyttelton had led a dangerously extravagant life.

Some were not surprised when they heard a strange tale — told several times by Thomas himself, and repeated endlessly by his circle of friends — about a ghostly visitor who had predicted his death.

It was said that the 35-year-old Lyttelton had been lying in bed in his London home on the night of November 24, 1779. He was woken just after midnight by what sounded like a bird fluttering at the curtains of his four-poster bed. The bleary-eyed Lord looked up to see a gaunt woman, dressed head-to-toe in white, standing close by. She looked at him with scorn, and pointed at him accusingly. Then, at last, she spoke.

The voice was a chilling, ghostly whisper – harsh and unearthly. "Hear me now, Thomas, Lord Lyttelton, for I have come to tell you that you will be dead within three days."

Then, in an instant, she had vanished.

❖

The apparition was so real that Lyttelton could not even pretend to himself that it had been a dream, and he was badly shaken by the experience. Soon, half of London had heard the tale. Lyttelton's friends rushed to reassure him, but his reckless lifestyle had made him many enemies. Those he had crossed or betrayed thought that the messenger was an emissary from Hell, come to give Lyttelton advance warning that the devil was due to collect his soul.

Everyone waited expectantly to see what would happen on November 27. Lyttelton himself woke with some trepidation. Still, he reassured himself, his health was good, so he should stop worrying. He decided to spend the day at Pit Place, a house he owned outside London, near Epsom in Surrey.

As the hours ticked by, Lyttelton grew increasingly

cheery. Darkness fell, and he sat down for dinner with several guests who had come to stay at the house. At the end of the meal he told his friends that he was sure he had beaten the ghost, and retired to bed with a smile and a wave.

But the day was not yet over. Lyttelton went to bed at 11:00pm. His manservant helped him undress and was then sent out to get a teaspoon. This man had been gone a mere minute, yet when he returned Lyttelton was writhing on the floor, in the grip of a fit. By midnight he was dead. His ghostly messenger had been right all along.

The story seems far-fetched, but may be true nevertheless – especially as so many people in London knew about the ghost's prediction before Lyttelton died. When he heard about Lyttelton's death, the famous writer Samuel Johnson called it the most extraordinary thing he had ever heard in his life.

"Tell them he killed me"

In 1977, Teresita Basa, a 48-year-old Filipino nurse was found stabbed to death in her Chicago apartment. Her jewels were missing, and police wearily concluded that the motive for her murder must have been robbery. But they also deduced that Miss Basa must have known her killer. There were no signs of forced entry into her home, so she must have opened the door to someone she knew.

It was a difficult case, and the police had few clues to work on. But, a couple of weeks after the murder, one of Teresita's hospital colleagues had a terrifying experience. Remy Chua, a fellow Filipino, was dozing in a locker room during a rest period when she became aware of someone standing close by. She opened her eyes and saw Teresita standing before her. She screamed, and ran from the room to tell fellow workers what had happened.

Over the next few weeks, Remy had several other visits from Teresita. She also saw the murdered woman in dreams, always with a male face close by. One day, in the hospital, she saw something that made her blood turn to ice. Standing in front of her was the man she had seen in these dreams. He was a hospital porter, and his name was Allan Showery. A few discreet inquiries revealed that he had been an acquaintance of Teresita Basa's.

Although she was convinced that it was Allan who had killed Teresita, Remy Chua had no evidence to prove it. She certainly could not waste the time of the busy Chicago police force with such a wild, implausible story. Still, the haunting continued. Now Teresita did not just appear to Remy in dreams or visions, she also seemed to speak through her. Remy began going into trances in which Teresita's voice seemed to come out of her mouth.

On one occasion, Teresita Basa's voice not only named Showery again as her killer, but also claimed that he had given jewels stolen from her appartment to his girlfriend. She went on to name various people who could identify her jewels, and even gave the telephone number of one of them. Then she said, in a voice full of pain and hurt: "Tell them Al came to fix my television, and then he killed me."

❖

If Remy Chua's husband had not been a doctor, the police might have dismissed the story out of hand. But Dr. Chua was too important a person to threaten with wasting police time. He himself had considered the matter long and hard before deciding to tell the police. When he did, they agreed to interview Allan Showery, but more out of desperation than anything else.

Interrogated by the police, Showery admitted he had promised Teresita Basa that he would fix her television. But he insisted he had never actually gone to her apartment. Police followed up the interview with a visit to Showery's girlfriend. They discovered she had a ring Showery had given her. Calling the phone number Remy Chua had given them, they found themselves talking to a cousin of the murdered woman. She was able to identify the ring as Teresita's. Showery was immediately arrested and charged with the killing.

The police always knew that a court case based on such sensational evidence was going to be difficult, and Showery protested his innocence and the ridiculousness of the case brought against him with great conviction. At the end of the trial, the jury could not reach a verdict, so a retrial was ordered. But before the second trial could begin, Showery changed his plea to guilty. He was sentenced to a total of 22 years in prison for murder and armed robbery.

This strange case is not entirely new in murder trials. Over the centuries, there have been several other stories of the ghosts of murder victims coming back from the grave to demand justice from their killers.

The Black Ribbon

Sir Marcus Beresford was surprised when his wife came down for breakfast one morning looking as white as a sheet, and with a black ribbon tied around her wrist. He asked what was the matter, but Lady Beresford refused to say. However, she did tell him that from now on she would always wear the black ribbon.

Sir Marcus was astounded. His wife was behaving very oddly. Furthermore, she seemed unnaturally anxious to know when the morning mail would arrive. He began to suspect that the mail might lead to an explanation for her strange conduct, and asked her if she was expecting a letter.

"I am," she replied. "I am expecting to hear that Lord Tyrone is dead."

Lord Tyrone was Lady Beresford's brother, and the two had always been very close, so it was no wonder she was so upset. Sir Marcus was flabbergasted, but tried to reassure his wife that she had just had a bad dream.

Yet sure enough, when the morning mail was delivered, there was a letter from Lord Tyrone's wife carrying news of his death.

❖

Lady Beresford never mentioned the events of that fateful morning again, and her husband, respecting her silence, never asked her about them, or about the black ribbon which she continued to wear.

And so life went on – at least for Lady Beresford. Sir Marcus died four years after Lord Tyrone. Lady Beresford married again, and had two daughters. Then, well into her forties, she had a son.

She was still in bed recovering from the birth when some friends came to visit. They found her looking ecstatically happy. The day also happened to be her birthday, and one of the guests congratulated her on reaching the age of 47.

Lady Beresford corrected her guest, telling him she was actually 48. However, he insisted that he was right, and told her that he had had a discussion about it with her mother earlier that day.

It turned out that Lady Beresford's mother had also thought her daughter was celebrating her 48th birthday. To see who was right, the guest had gone to the parish registry to look up the date of Lady Beresford's birth, and so he could assure her that she was, in fact, only 47.

There was an awkward silence after the guest finished speaking. The guests all expected Lady Beresford to be happy to find she was a year younger, so they were taken aback by her reaction. She looked thunderstruck.

"Sir," said Lady Beresford eventually, in a quiet, dejected voice, "you have signed my death warrant." Then she asked everyone to leave.

Embarrassed and perplexed, the guests trooped out of the room. But as they wished her goodbye, Lady Beresford asked one of them, her close friend Lady Betty Cobb, to stay behind.

The door closed, and the two women were left by themselves. Only then did Lady Beresford explain why the discovery of her true age had affected her so deeply.

She revealed that one night many years previously, her beloved brother, Lord Tyrone, had appeared in her bedroom just before dawn and told her that he was dead. He also foretold the death of Sir Marcus, and added that Lady Beresford would marry again and give birth to two daughters and a son, before dying herself at 47.

Lady Beresford had thought she was having a

terrible dream, but the apparition told her that she was awake. Still incredulous, she asked it to prove that it was real. Its response was to touch her lightly on the wrist.

The apparition's hand, Lady Beresford told her startled friend, had felt as cold as marble, and where its fingers had touched her skin, her flesh had withered. She added that the apparition had begged her never to let a living soul see her injury, and that was why she had tied the black ribbon around her wrist.

All the apparition's predictions, except for Lady Beresford's death, had since come true. And one more thing made Lady Beresford convinced that she had really seen Lord Tyrone. In their youth, she and her brother had made a secret pact that whichever of them died first would try to come back after death to visit the survivor.

Lady Cobb tried to reassure her friend, telling her that the birth had left her exhausted and that she needed to rest. She kissed Lady Beresford lightly on the forehead and left the room, telling her to ring the bell by her bedside if she needed anything.

An hour later, Lady Cobb was sitting dozing on a chair when she was startled to hear the urgent ringing of a small handbell. She hurried to her friend's room, but by the time she got there, Lady Beresford was dead.

Remembering her friend's strange story, Lady Cobb could not help herself. She picked up Lady

Beresford's lifeless wrist, and untied the black ribbon. Sure enough, her wrist was withered in just the way she had described.

Lady Beresford's black ribbon is said to have remained with the Cobb family. Indeed, they may still have it to this day.

The Tedworth Drummer

In 17th-century England, civil war swept across the land, leaving ruin and bloodshed in its wake. Troubled times bring troubled minds and, in the midst of this uncertainty, strange sects emerged. People believed witches and wizards with mysterious powers stalked the land, and demons and devils haunted the still country nights. This was especially true of the inhabitants of the Wiltshire village of Tedworth, now called North Tidworth, and perhaps they had good reason... For almost a year, the home of a respectable magistrate was disturbed by strange noises, mysterious lights, and objects that seemed to move with a power of their own.

The magistrate was named John Mompesson, and it was whispered that he had brought the trouble on himself. One day in March 1662, he went to the nearby town of Ludgershall on court business. Here, he was disturbed by the sound of drumming in the street outside. Mompesson summoned an aide.

"Who is making that infernal racket?" he asked. "It is interfering with the business of this court."

The aide replied, "It's a wandering musician by the name of William Drury, sir. He has been banging on his drum for several days now, much to our annoyance. It seems he is a soldier of the King who is now infirm. He has an official permit which gives him the right to beg for money in the street."

This was unusual, for at the time most beggars were treated with great cruelty. It was not uncommon for them to be flogged, or even branded with red-hot irons, to drive them away from a town.

Mompesson stood up and looked at Drury through the window. "Infirm, is he? He looks like a pretty sturdy beggar to me. Have him brought before me."

So it was that John Mompesson first met William Drury. The drummer immediately produced his permit, but Mompesson quickly realized it was a forgery. He had Drury arrested, and ordered an official to take away his drum. Drury was released the next day, lucky not to have been flogged or branded. His real punishment was the loss of his drum. Despite Drury's angry protests, Mompesson would not allow him to have it back. Instead, it was sent on to the magistrate's home.

❖

The drum arrived just as Mompesson was leaving his large, handsome manor house to travel to London on business. He stayed in the capital for a couple of weeks, but on his return he found his home in turmoil. He was walking up the path when a servant came out to greet him.

"Oh sir," she sighed, "the whole household has had no sleep all night. No sooner had we settled down to our beds than there came a strange banging. We thought at once it must be men come to break into the house, but no one could be seen. And banging and knockings were heard until first light."

Mompesson knew this woman well, and trusted her. He was puzzled by her story, and could offer no explanation.

"Well, my dear lady," he said, "let us prepare ourselves, in case our phantom knocker returns."

The household did not have to wait for long. Three nights later, the knocking came again. Mompesson was ready. He seized a pair of pistols and hurried to the room where the noises were coming from. He flung back the door and found – absolutely nothing. Then the noises started again, somewhere else in the house. Mompesson rushed from room to room, but all of them he found empty. He was beginning to feel increasingly puzzled and angry. Who could it be, he wondered, who could be running around inside his house and making all this mischief?

Then, the sounds moved outside the building. At first, they seemed to be coming from the roof, but then they moved higher, rising slowly into the air above the house, before fading away to silence. Whoever was making the noise seemed to possess the power of invisibility.

Over the next month, the Mompesson family grew used to these bizarre bangings. The noises were sometimes loud enough to wake up the entire village. Now, whenever the family was visited by their ghostly noise-maker, the pattern remained the same. The sound would start somewhere outside the house, and then move inside, usually settling in the room where William Drury's drum was kept. The start of events would be heralded by a strange whirring noise above the house, and then a banging, which witnesses described as a hollow, thumping sound, would begin. After this, the family would hear drumming: not just odd beats, but whole tunes, played as well as they would have been by any regimental drummer.

The noises would continue for maybe two hours or more, then suddenly stop. The house would be troubled in this way for four or five nights in a row, and then there would be three days of peace before the bangings started again.

❖

The Mompessons were at their wits end, for the whole household found it impossible to sleep when the ghostly drummer came to visit. John Mompesson was especially anxious for his wife, who was expecting a baby. As he feared, the drummer came on the night of the birth. But strangely enough, the noises sounded quieter than usual, and for the following three weeks, the family enjoyed complete peace. For the moment, at least, it seemed that whatever was causing the noise meant the new baby no harm.

But then the ghost came back, and this time the hauntings were worse than ever. It seemed to have grown bored with just making noises. Instead, it turned its attention to Mompessons' two elder daughters, who were 7 and 11. It visited the room where they slept together, and lifted their beds up into the air as they lay sleeping. On one occasion, hearing the screams of his terrified daughters, Mompesson rushed to their room and saw their bed frames shaking so violently that he thought the beds would fall to pieces.

The girls' beds were immediately moved to the attic. This was an area of the house that had previously been untroubled by the ghost. But it followed them up there. Mompesson now did the only thing left to do – he called for the local priest, in the hope that he could banish the phantom with the power of prayer.

Far from driving the ghost away, however, the sight of the priest seemed to excite it to even greater acts of mischief. On his first visit, the astounded cleric was subjected to a terrifying display of its most spectacular tricks. Before the eyes of this man, and several members of Mompesson's household, chairs walked around the room, the children's shoes flew through the air, and everything else in the house that wasn't nailed down started to fidget and stir. A piece of wood from a bed even struck the priest's leg, though fortunately it did not hit him hard enough to hurt him.

❖

By now, word of the happenings at Tedworth had spread throughout the country. Stories even reached the newly crowned king, Charles II, in London. He and his queen each sent their own courtiers to investigate. But both visited the Mompesson's home on a day when the phantom was resting, and went away disappointed.

Another observer, however, had better luck. His name was Joseph Glanvill, a 26-year-old clergyman who had recently left Oxford University. In later life, Glanvill became a founding member of the Royal Society, an association set up to encourage scientific investigation. He was a rational, level-headed, and highly intelligent man, not given to wild superstitions or imaginings. He made his own trip to Tedworth, and gave a detailed account of what he saw while he was there.

On the night of Glanvill's stay, the Mompesson children were sent to bed at 8:00pm. A little while later, a servant came down to say that the ghostly drummer had arrived in their room. Glanvill, Mompesson and another man went upstairs to investigate. Even before they reached the bedroom, they could hear an odd scratching noise. Inside the room, it became obvious that the noise was coming from behind the bolster at the head of the girls' bed. At first Glanvill wondered if it was the girls somehow making the knocking, but he could clearly see both their hands outside the bedclothes. Then, he put his arm down behind the bolster to try to find what was causing the noise, but the sound simply shifted to another part of the bed.

The strange noises went on like this for another half hour, then moved to beneath the mattress. Now, instead of scratching, there seemed to be panting sounds, rather like a dog out of breath. The noise grew louder and louder, until the doors and windows began to shake. By this time the girls had fled to another room, but those still in the bedroom began to fear for their lives.

In the midst of the cacophony, out of the corner of his eye, Glanvill saw a movement in a linen bag. The bag was hanging from a post of the bed. Thinking there must be a mouse inside, he grabbed the bag. But, when he opened it, he found that it was empty.

After this, the noises abruptly ceased, and the exhausted men went to bed. However more was yet to come. Early next morning, Glanvill was awoken by a loud knocking on the door. When he opened the door, there was no one there. Then, after breakfast, when he went to collect his horse, he found it disturbed and sweating, as though it had been ridden throughout the night. It fell lame on the journey home and died a couple of days later.

❖

The haunting reached a climax in the early winter months of November and December 1662. There were disturbances at the Mompesson house almost every night. Then the family had a lucky break. They had long suspected that William Drury was responsible for their troubles, and now they learned that he had been arrested for stealing pigs. He was imprisoned in Gloucester, 100km (60 miles) away.

A prison officer, who was a friend of the Mompessons, overheard Drury talking to another inmate. Drury had discovered that this man came from Wiltshire, and asked him if he had heard any news of strange goings-on at Tedworth. Naturally, like everyone else in the county, this man had heard of the hauntings, and filled Drury in on the details. The story had been exaggerated somewhat in its frequent telling, and the man told Drury that the devil himself appeared to float above the Mompesson household, beating a drum so loudly that the noise shook the leaves from the branches of the trees that surrounded the house. Drury smiled a smug smile, and boasted that he had been "plaguing" the family. John Mompesson, Drury claimed, would have no peace until he had been sufficiently punished for taking the drum.

The Tedworth Drummer

The disturbances seemed to stop while Drury was in prison. The whole Mompesson family breathed a sign of relief when they heard that Drury was to be transported to America, as punishment for his pig stealing. But they had not heard the last of him yet. Before the sentence could be carried out, Drury escaped from the jail at Gloucester, and soon the hauntings began again.

By now, the Mompesson family had grown so used to the hauntings that they almost took these strange events in their stride. The spirit too, at times, seemed almost playful rather than malicious. Once, a servant saw a wooden board moving across the children's bedroom. Realizing that the ghost was at work, the servant asked it to give him the board, which eerily moved toward him. A game of push-and-pull followed. The servant thrust away the board, only to have the spirit shove it forward again. This went on about 20 times, until Mompesson arrived and told the man to stop.

But the ghost could be vicious too. It started picking on a fat servant named John. It would disturb him almost every night, pulling all the bedclothes off his bed. Sometimes, servant and spirit would have a tug-of-war over the bedclothes. The village blacksmith, intrigued by these goings on, volunteered to spend a night in John's room. He got very little sleep, as he felt the ghost tweaking his nose with what seemed like red hot pincers.

Only one thing seemed to frighten the ghost – a

drawn sword or a pistol. It seemed to be frightened of getting hurt. It may have had good reason to be afraid. One time, when John Mompesson saw some logs moving by his fireplace, he fired a pistol at them. Later, he found drops of fresh blood on the hearth and on the stairs outside the room.

As time went by, the ghost seemed to develop a voice. Strange cries of "A witch, a witch..." were heard coming from the girls' bedroom. And, after almost a year of invisible haunting, the ghost seemed to be trying to summon the energy to make itself visible. Mompesson once glimpsed a shadowy figure moving up the main staircase of the house. On another occasion, a servant woke to find a looming shape, with two red, glaring eyes, staring at him as he lay in his bed.

But the end of the haunting was near. William Drury was eventually tracked down and arrested at his home village of Uffcott in Wiltshire. Mompesson brought charges of witchcraft against him, and he was put on trial at Salisbury. He was found "not guilty", as Mompesson could find no conclusive evidence to link him directly with the bizarre events at Tedworth. But, nonetheless, justice had finally caught up with William Drury. His earlier sentence of transportation for pig-stealing still stood, and he was shipped out of England, bound for America, in 1663. From that time on, no more was heard either of him or of his ghostly accomplices.

Afterwards

The Tedworth drummings were one of the best observed and authenticated of all hauntings. They were experienced by dozens of people, from family and servants, to local landowners, church ministers, and independent observers. Almost all these witnesses blamed the disturbances on witchcraft. It was not thought that Drury himself was a witch, but one report said that he had been given a book of spells by "an odd fellow, who was counted a wizard".

Today, this seems like an implausible tale, but there is no more likely or convincing explanation as to what happened at the Mompesson's house. Three hundred years later, the secret of the Tedworth Drummer remains as mysterious as ever.

The House that Ghosts Built

In San José, California, back in the 1890s, it was inevitable that Sarah Winchester would be the subject of incessant gossip. She was, after all, one of America's richest widows. She was also deeply eccentric. Talk was that she sat down in the dining room of her huge mansion at the stroke of midnight, and ate dinner with 12 ghosts. Not that you could see them, of course; they were *invisible* guests... but places were laid for them around the imposing dining table, and she would converse with them long into the night. When not eating with these spirits, she would talk to them in a specially designed, windowless "séance room" in the house. And what messages did these spirits bring? Was it news of her departed loved ones? Was it a glimpse into events in the future? No, what the spirits told Sarah Winchester was: "Build, build, build!"

And build she did. That much at least was true.

Full of secret passageways, hidden entrances, stairs that lead to nowhere and doors that open to nothing, Sarah's residence, Winchester House, is one of the strangest buildings in the world. Any visitor would tell you this rambling mansion had been conceived by a tormented and haunted mind. But no wonder, for the tale of its creation is a tragic one.

❖

Winchester House had its genesis in 1862, when Sarah Pardee of New Haven, Connecticut, married William Winchester, the heir to the Winchester rifle fortune. The rifle, known as "the gun that won the West", was one of the most popular weapons of its day, and it had played a major part in the defeat of the Native Americans in the 19th century.

William and Sarah, who settled on the East coast, found themselves sharing one of the largest inheritances in America. But, as so often happens, money did not buy them happiness. Sarah had a child who died within a week of its birth. The death caused such anguish to the couple that they had no other children. Then William Winchester caught tuberculosis. After a long illness he died in 1881, leaving Sarah a 40-year-old widow with twenty million dollars – so much money she hardly knew what to do with it.

In her grief, Sarah turned to spiritualism, hoping to find consolation in the "mediums" who claim to have the power to bring messages from the dead back to the living. But the first medium she consulted brought not comfort, but dread. In an eerie ceremony Sarah would remember for the rest of her life, the medium, a small, birdlike woman, ushered her into a neat room, late one autumn afternoon. In the fading light, the woman held her hand and, with flickering eyes and vacant expression, she spoke in a clear, steady voice.

"There is a curse upon your family, Sarah Winchester. Your pain and torment is a punishment visited on you by hostile spirits killed by the Winchester rifle. There are many thousands of such sorry souls, and they all wish you ill…"

Sarah, so terrified she could hardly speak, managed to stammer out: "What can I do?"

The medium's answer was a bizarre one. "There is only one way to counter the curse that has fallen upon you. You must build and build and build and build… for the rest of your life."

Such advice seemed no more or less crazy than anything else Sarah had heard that afternoon. If that was what she must do to avoid further misfortune, then that was what she would do.

❖

In 1884, three years after her husband's death, Sarah moved out to California, and bought an eight-room farmstead in San José. From the time she arrived until her death 38 years later, carpenters and builders were employed seven days a week, 24 hours a day, extending the house until it became a massive mansion the size of a sprawling village. By the time she died, the house had 160 rooms spread over four floors, 17 chimneys, 40 staircases, 467 doorways and over 1,000 windows.

Yet even those figures do not reflect the full extent of Sarah Winchester's mania for building. At one time, the mansion was topped by turrets and lookouts that rose seven floors high. But in 1906, the house was struck by the great San Francisco earthquake. Sarah was trapped inside the devastated mansion for several hours, and fearing more quakes to come, she reduced the house to its current four floors to make it safer.

She felt her narrow escape in the earthquake had been a warning, and took to building more and more rooms with even greater desperation. As space ran out and further extensions became impractical, she ordered rooms to be constructed and then knocked down again, as part of her constant quest to keep the builders busy. If these vanished building projects had all survived, the Winchester House would have had an unimaginable 750 rooms.

Despite her great wealth, Sarah Winchester did not bother to employ an architect to design her ever-growing house. She did it all herself. She would sketch out plans on paper, or even tablecloths, and then hand them to a foreman. He would see to it that the work was carried out by a team of a dozen or so builders.

Curiously, although Sarah had no training as an architect, some of her ideas were way ahead of her time. She patented a design for sinks with scrubbing boards and soap holders, and also pioneered the idea of indoor cranks to open outdoor shutters. The mansion's 47 fireplaces had hinged drops for collecting ashes, and the gas lighting was operated by a simple, innovative push-button system. With millions of dollars to burn, Sarah Winchester always insisted her workmen did a quality job.

❖

As the years went by, Sarah began to lose touch with reality altogether, and her designs took on weirder and weirder forms. Columns would be installed upside down, rooms were built inside rooms, and skylights were placed indoors where no sunlight could reach them. Doors opened onto blank walls or sheer drops. One chimney rose through four floors, and then stopped just inches from the roof, making the fireplace underneath it unusable.

Strangest of all were the mansion's staircases. One climbed up to a ceiling and stopped. Another took seven separate flights and 44 steps to rise a mere 3m (10ft). But some of Sarah's designs were not as strange as they looked. Tiny doorways less than 1.5m (5ft) high may have been small for most people, but she was only 1.47m (4ft 10in) herself, and could walk through them without stooping. Stairs she installed, with steps only 5cm (2in) high, might have been designed to help ease the pain of arthritis, which plagued her later years.

Over nearly four decades of building, the residents of San José were treated to a constantly evolving spectacle. It was no wonder that some of the visitors to the strange labyrinth would conclude the building's true architects were Sarah's ghostly friends, and Winchester House was a "a spook palace" designed by the dead. Only Sarah knew for sure, and she took this final mystery to the grave in 1922.

Afterwards

Sarah Winchester's mansion still stands today, where, known as the "Winchester Mystery House", it is one of California's top tourist attractions. The visitors who flock to see it are promised "rambling roofs and exquisite hand–inlaid parquet floors… gold and silver chandeliers and Tiffany art glass windows". They are assured they will be "impressed by the staggering amount of creativity, energy, and expense poured into each and every detail". Perhaps Sarah would be pleased to know that her remarkably extravagant obsession is still intriguing and mystifying thousands of visitors, a whole eight decades after her death brought a halt to this extraordinary creation.

Also from Usborne True Stories

TRUE STORIES
OF
HEROES

Paul Dowswell

His blood ran cold and Perevozchenko
was seized by panic. He knew that his
body was absorbing lethal doses of
radiation, but instead of fleeing he
stayed to search for his colleague.
Peering into the dark through a
broken window that overlooked the
reactor hall, he could see only a mass
of tangled wreckage.

   By now he had absorbed so much
radiation he felt as if his whole body
was on fire. But then he remembered
that there were several other men near
to the explosion who might also be
trapped...

From firefighters battling with a blazing nuclear
reactor to a helicopter rescue team on board a fast-
sinking ship, this is an amazingly vivid collection of
stories about men and women whose extraordinary
courage has captured the imagination of millions.

TRUE SURVIVAL STORIES

Paul Dowswell

As he fell through the floor Griffiths instinctively grabbed at the bombsight with both hands, but an immense gust of freezing air sucked the rest of his body out of the aircraft. With the wind and the throb of the Boston's two engines roaring in his ears, he found himself halfway out of the plane, legs and lower body pressed hard against the fuselage. He yelled at the top of his voice: "Geeeerrrooooowwww!!!!", but knew immediately that there was almost no chance his crewmate could hear him.

From shark attacks and blazing airships to exploding spacecraft and sinking submarines, these are real stories of people who have stared death in the face and lived to tell the tale. Find out what separates the living from the dead when catastrophe strikes.

TRUE SPY STORIES

Paul Dowswell

"In all your years of fame," Kramer
explained delicately, "you have known
some of the most powerful men in
Europe. Would you consider returning to
Paris now to mingle again with these
influential gentlemen? And, while you're
doing this, might you be able to keep me
informed of anything interesting they
might say?"
Margaretha looked curious but non-
committal.
Kramer went on, "We could pay you well
for this information — say 24,000 francs."

What are real spies like? Some, like beautiful Mata
Hari, are every bit as glamorous as famous fictional
agents such as James Bond. But spies usually live
shadowy double lives, risking prison, torture and
execution for a chance to change history.

TRUE ESCAPE STORIES

Paul Dowswell

Finally, the night had come to take a trip to the roof. Morris spent the day beforehand trying to curb his restlessness. What if the way up to the roof was blocked? What if the ventilator motor had been replaced after all? All their painstaking work would be wasted. The 12 year sentence stretched out before him. Then another awful thought occurred. The holes in the wall would be discovered eventually, and that would mean even more years added on to his sentence.

As well as locked doors, high walls and barbed wire, many escaping prisoners also face savage dogs and armed guards who shoot to kill. From Alcatraz to Devil's Island, read the extraordinary tales of people who risked their lives for their freedom.